Born of Inward Dreamings

Volume One:

Gothica

A collection of short stories, exploring the mysterious, supernatural, otherworldly, and the darkness that resides within us.

By Gareth Meadows

Rapacious Publishing

First published in Great Britain in 2022 by
Rapacious Publishing (via Amazon KDP)
All stories © Gareth Meadows 2022
Cover art by Gareth Meadows
Edited by Jonathan Oliver

An abridged version of the story 'My, What Big Teeth You Have' was originally published in Fudoki Magazine, October 26th, 2021

The rights of the author of this work have been asserted by them in accordance with the Copyright, Designs and Patents Act, 1988.

All rights reserved. No parts of this publication may be reproduced or transmitted, in any form or by any means, electronic or mechanical, including photocopy, recording, or any information storage and retrieval system, without permission in writing from the publisher.

This book is a work of fiction. Names and characters, businesses, organisations, places, and events are either the product of the author's imagination or are used fictitiously. Any resemblance to actual persons, living or dead, events or locales is entirely coincidental.

"Love is like death, it must come to us all, but to each his own unique way and time. Sometimes it will be avoided, but never can it be cheated, and never will it be forgotten."

JACOB GRIMM

CONTENTS

Beyond the Seventh Fall 9

Hoard 57

Mirror, Mirror 87

The Beast Must Die 105

My, What Big Teeth You Have 139

The Watcher 147

A Noble Heart Must Answer 189

Forlorn 215

Of Older and Fouler Things 265

El Caleuche 295

Beyond the Seventh Fall

Once upon a time...

There are many tales of the damsel princess, locked away for all eternity by a wicked queen. These stories pass into folklore, or as bedtime tales for our children, but that is all they are – works of fiction, designed to enthral, and shock young minds.

As is the case with most folk tales, there exists a kernel of truth in their origin, even if the moral is lost in translation from generation to generation.

There is a reason why people tell stories. Sometimes, it is simply to entertain, other times, to provide a stark warning. Beware! Because the things in the darkness are real. Sometimes those things *are* the darkness. And humanity is nought but the guttering light of a candle, holding back an ocean of iniquity. Those things are drawn to the light, waiting for the nub to finally burn out, thus allowing them to overwhelm everything pure, and decent, and good.

But that is a tale for another time. Right now, our focus is on the age-old tale of the poor, unfortunate princess, under the thrall of a wicked, deceitful witch.

Pay attention to children's stories, dear reader, particularly the things they do not say. Look for their commonalities, then cast your naturally cynical adult eye over them and you may just spy the golden nugget of truth that lies at the tale's heart.

"Once upon a time, there was a princess. Fair of face and heart, with skin as pale as snow, lips as red as rubies, and hair the dark of ebony…"

Gawain had heard the story a thousand times before from his father and mother, who heard it from their parents, who had heard it from their parents, who, in turn, had heard it from their parents, and so ad infinitum. He could recite it verbatim, though he had learned to add his own embellishments over time that made it uniquely his.

Gawain was fifteen and had long since considered himself too old to be concerned with common fairy tales – he was far too cultured and sophisticated to believe such things. And yet, he relished relaying these tales to his young nephew and niece and found the stories came back to him with ease. He even did the voices, in much the way that his father had brought these tales to life when he was an infant. And Willem and Cecille adored their uncle and relished story time above all other things.

"What became of the poor princess, Uncle Gawain?" asked Cecille, pulling the bedsheets around her neck.

"Oh, she's still locked in her tower, Cecille," he told her. "Stuck in unending sleep for all eternity, until she can be rescued from her prison by the bravest, most courageous knight in all the land."

"You mean someone like you, Uncle Gawain?" asked Willem.

For a moment, Gawain was glad of the flickering candlelight to disguise his blushing cheeks. He may have exaggerated his prowess as a warrior to his impressionable charges. Truth be told, he had never experienced more than practice sparring with wooden training swords, and he was average at best at that. Though he got the better of his closest friend, Robert, almost every time.

"Um, I think that's enough story time for tonight," he rallied. "You two need to get some sleep before your parents get home."

"Awwww!"

"Shush now. If you don't go to sleep, your maman and papa might not let me sit with you again. And then we'll all be in trouble."

The pair instantly threw themselves down in their beds, pulling their sheets around them, eyes screwed shut in mock sleep.

"Goodnight, little ones," grinned Gawain. He blew out the candle and let himself out of their bedroom.

"They're not wrong, you know," cackled an old, rasping voice.

"Grandfather," gasped Gawain, his heart skipping a beat as he spun to find the old man hiding in the landing's gloom. "What are you doing here?"

"I came to see *you*, boy," said Sanson Bedeau – the Bedeau family's oldest surviving member – warmly clamping his hand on his grandson's shoulder. "You never visit me anymore."

"I'm sorry, Grandfather," replied Gawain. "I've just been so busy."

"I know, I know," chuckled Sanson. "Too busy for an old fart like me. Come, come."

He led Gawain downstairs and into the kitchen, where he unstoppered a flagon of red wine. The rich, fruity aroma filled the room as his grandfather poured them each a cup.

"None for me, thank you," demurred Gawain. "Maman would not approve."

"Then it's a damn good job she isn't here," said the old man, handing him the wooden cup. Gawain took it, and Sanson tapped his own against it, before downing a large gulp and taking a seat at the small, round dining table.

Gawain sipped at his drink. It was strong and slightly sour, though not unpleasant. In fact, the more he tried it, the tastier it became.

His papa, Estiene, was not a wealthy man. As a career soldier, serving king and country his whole life, he had made a good living. However, killing other men was not as lucrative as the shiny armour and weapons would have many believe. Yet, they were certainly better off than many, and Gawain and his older brother, Aymon, had never known an empty stomach. However, there was something missing from Gawain's life. It lacked flavour – *excitement.*

"When are you going to leave this place and make your way in the world, boy?" scolded Sanson, from nowhere. "You are almost a man. You're taller than me – taller than your papa even – and more of a man than that brother of yours will ever be. What are you waiting for?"

Gawain shrugged. His grandfather was not wrong – he already towered over every other member of his family. He was fair-featured and broad-shouldered, with glossy chestnut hair that seemed to fall effortlessly into style no matter what he did with it. Gawain longed to go out and see the world, make his fortune, and live out the adventures his grandfather and father had boasted of all his young life.

"I'm not sure, Grandfather," he replied, eventually. "I… Maman doesn't—"

"Is your maman living your life for you, boy? Is she going to go out to work for you? Is she going to raise your children? Cook your meals forever? You'll end up as wet and useless as your brother. I was at war when I was your age. Had I not been, I would have been off seeking the legend."

"The legend?" snorted Gawain. He had heard this tune a thousand times. "You mean the princess in the tower?"

"Yes, the princess in the tower!" snapped the old man. "You know full well that's what I mean."

"But, Grandfather, it's just a children's story," chuckled Gawain. "You know that."

The old man leaned forward, lowering his voice, conspiratorially. "It is *not* just a story," he whispered. "The directions are in the tale. You know the words."

"'Towards the setting sun, beyond the woods and past the mountains, beyond the seventh fall, there lies a fortress'," intoned Gawain, in mock, sing-song dramatism. "'And in the tallest room of the tallest tower, the princess slumbers in eternal, cursed sleep. There she waits, for the bravest and most hardy – her one true love – to free her from the foul hex with a single, sweet kiss.'"

"You can sneer all you like, boy," snarled his grandfather, "but I happen to know this legend is true."

"Really?" grinned Gawain. "I think you should put the wine down, Grandfather." He giggled and hiccoughed. He was starting to feel a little giddy.

"Ah, there is something I have never told you," whispered Sanson. "When I was a little younger than you are now, I accompanied my older brother in search of the legend."

"Wait… what? You have a brother?"

"I *had* a brother," confirmed the old man. "His name was Tumas. We followed the story's directions – we headed west, through the forest, along the mountain pass, and beyond the falls. It took us three days, but in the end, we found it. Atop another peak, just a stone's throw away, there stood an abandoned fortress, just as the legend describes."

"And then what?" asked Gawain, intrigued despite his teenage cynicism.

"And then nothing," shrugged Sanson. "We turned back and went home. My brother was curious to see if the place existed. However, Tumas did not want to bring me into danger. And so, we returned home. Then, just a few days later, Tumas left — in the midst of night — and I never saw him again."

"You mean?"

"I believe so," nodded Sanson. "He told no-one where he was going, so I could only surmise. Though I could not share my suspicions with my parents, lest I would never have been able to follow his journey."

"What? You went after him?"

"No. We both knew the risks. Death awaited most who follow the legend – after all, many have sought out the princess, though none have succeeded. And keep in mind, I heard this tale from my papa, who heard it from his papa, who heard it from his papa. How many have tried their hand? How many have failed? And yet, I believed myself more worthy, more capable than Tumas. I intended to return to the fortress the following summer, giving my parents time to grieve my brother. But war came and I answered my country's call. By the time I returned home, I had grown old and weary. Instead, I married, and I raised children of my own. I never did follow my destiny."

Just then the timber-framed house's back door opened and Aymon and his wife, Collette, arrived home.

"Good evening," said Collette. "How were the children? Did they behave for you, Gawain?"

"They were fine, as always," replied Gawain. He did not like his brother's wife. Becoming a parent filled her with the sense that she was mother to the world and, as such, could tell everyone what to do and how to live their lives. She glanced at the cup of wine in his hand and raised a disapproving eyebrow but said nothing.

"You filling his head with nonsense again, Grandfather?" grinned Aymon. The old man only scowled in response.

*

Soon after, Gawain departed for his home on the other side of their village, accompanied by his grandfather. There was a warm glow in his chest, and his head was fuzzy from the wine, but he was in good cheer as he and the old man joked and jibed on their journey home.

"This is me," said Sanson as he arrived at the lane which led to his small cottage, where he had lived alone since the passing of Gawain's much-beloved grandmother. He embraced Gawain, though the old man never tried to hide that his grandson was his favourite. He broke the clinch and then reached into his pocket and brandished a folded piece of yellowed parchment.

"Take this," he ordered, pushing the square of heavy paper into Gawain's hand.

"What is it?"

"It's a map," whispered Sanson. "Drawn by my brother some fifty years ago."

"To the fortress?" smiled Gawain, playing along with the old man's folly.

"Yes, to the fortress," snapped Sanson. "The rhyme tells you part of the tale, but you need the map to lead you to the valley. Many have gone in search and failed to find the way."

"Okay, thank you, Grandfather," said Gawain, resisting the urge to roll his eyes. "Good night."

As he turned to walk away, the old man gripped his wrist and held him back.

"I know you think I'm crazy," said Sanson. "Full of fanciful tales and nonsense. But I implore you to heed my words, Gawain. This legend is true. I *know* it! And I believe our family are destined to break the curse, free the princess from her imprisonment, and restore her to her rightful place on the throne. I lost my chance, but it's not too late for you, Gawain. I feel it in my heart! Don't ask me how, I just do."

There was something in his grandfather's voice – in his eyes. A vehemence. A certainty. A burning inferno of absolute certitude that made Gawain hesitate and the hackles rise on his neck. He embraced the old man again, then made his way home.

As he climbed into bed, Gawain metaphorically shook himself free from the spectre of a thousand-year-old fairy tale. Of course it was not true! It was just the fancy of a silly old man who liked to tease his grandchildren. Yet still, before he snuffed out his candle, he reached for the parchment, unfolded it, and looked over the old hand-drawn map.

It was just as his grandfather had described, depicting the forest, the mountains, the valley pass with the seven waterfalls, and the fortress, in the top right corner. And a dotted line depicting the journey from his home village to the legendary destination.

Gawain shook his head, grinning, and refolded the parchment. He blew out the candle and settled into almost instant sleep.

Gawain woke with a start, sweat beading his brow, running down the back of his nightshirt, and pooling in his lower back, making him shiver despite the warmth of the summer night.

The butterflies of dreams flitted through his conscious mind, evading capture, just beyond reach. Only fragments stayed with him: the forest, a desperate fight, a flurry of teeth and claws – and worse things, hiding from his memory, though the fear was all too real. And then, the fortress: a stark silhouette against a leaden sky, the faint rumble of thunder threatening to burst the clouds and release their chilly payload. And finally, a spiral staircase, seemingly without end, its wedge, stone steps even and defined – tapering from wide enough to accommodate a full foot to just a couple of inches at their narrowest point, making them treacherous to any errantly-placed boot. The climb culminated at a varnished wooden door, heavy and imposing, as if untouched by the passage of time. Gawain had pushed at it, and it easily swung open…

…and that is where he woke.

It was still dark outside, though the eastern horizon was fringed with purples, oranges, and blues, as Gawain quickly dressed, pulled on his boots, and stuffed his grandfather's map into his pocket. He snuck downstairs, careful not to wake his parents, as he loaded a pack with enough food to last several days if he was careful. Finally, he found two empty wineskins and strapped them to his belt. He would fill them from the village well before he departed.

Just minutes later, he stood outside Robert's parents' single-storey cottage. He and Robert had been inseparable since they were old enough to talk, and Gawain could not imagine embarking on an adventure such as this without his best friend for company. He followed the cottage's boundary wall until he located the correct room, then tapped on the glass pane until he saw movement beyond, finally approaching the small window. The figure peered through the glass, then pushed it open.

"Gawain?" yawned Robert. "What are you doing here? What time is it?"

Robert was a short, stout, round-faced young man, with soft, pudgy features and sausage-like fingers. He gave the impression of someone destined to be fat, even though he was not particularly overweight. That did not stop the village's other youngsters, particularly the girls, from teasing him. The boys would not do so in Gawain's presence as he was notoriously quick to anger where his best friend was concerned, and whilst he might have reservations about raising his hand to a girl, he had no such compunction when it came to other boys. Many a rival had found themselves on the wrong end of Gawain's fists over the years for making cruel comments about Robert.

"Get some clothes on, grab enough food for a few days and meet me outside in five minutes," whispered Gawain.

"What? Why?" protested Robert.

"Just do it."

A few minutes later, Robert staggered around the corner, rubbing his eyes, and struggling to keep an overloaded satchel on his narrow shoulder.

"What in god's name have you got in there?" snorted Gawain.

"You said to bring enough food for a few days," protested Robert.

"How many people did you think you would be feeding?" Gawain lifted the satchel's strap and peered inside. "Is that a full ham?"

"It's cooked," said Robert. "Leftovers from last night."

Gawain sighed, took his friend's satchel strap, and lifted it over his head, so it ran diagonally across his chest. "Better?" he asked. Robert nodded and smiled.

The village was bathed in pale, early morning light as Gawain led his friend between the jumble of houses until they arrived at his grandfather's place. However, instead of needing to knock at the door to wake the old man, they found Sanson already sat on the bench beside his cottage's entrance, smoking his pipe.

"Good morning, Gawain," called Sanson. "Morning, Robert."

"Grandfather?"

"Morning, Monsieur Bedeau," greeted Robert.

"You're waiting for me?" asked Gawain. "How did you know?"

"You had the dream," said Sanson. It was a statement, not a question.

"How did you know?"

"So did I," replied the old man. "The night before I first made the journey with Tumas, all those years ago. And many, many times since. And when I woke, Tumas had had the same dream. From that moment, I *knew* it was real. She is reaching out to us from her dream world, calling for us to rescue her. It is too late for me, Gawain. *You* must answer the call."

The old man reached to the pack beside him, lifted it with some effort and handed it to Gawain. It clanked as the contents shifted. Poking from the top were two swords.

"Weapons, a small axe for firewood, ropes and climbing equipment," Sanson told him. "You will need them. Good luck, both of you."

"Um, where are we going?" asked Robert.

"I'll tell you on the way," Gawain explained. He helped his grandfather to his feet and hugged him one final time.

"Let's go," he said, and he and Robert headed west, towards the forest canopy, which was a dark blotch on the distant horizon, the peaks of mountains protruding into the lightening sky.

***

He sprinted through the bracken, weaving through the trees, bramble barbs lashing at his shins and snatching at his arms, with Robert in close step behind him. Further back, the thing smashed through the undergrowth, barrelling after them like a furious ball of dark fur, teeth, and claws.

Gawain grabbed Robert and pulled him behind a tree, and the pair stood there, panting, chests heaving, and hearts thudding so hard that Gawain feared the sound might give them away. The noise of their pursuer faded – had it lost them?

"What the bloody hell was that?" gasped Robert.

"Shhhhh!" hissed Gawain. It was still out there. He could hear it snuffling – trying to pick up their scent. He peered around the tree trunk, to see if he could find the beast without making himself known. And there it was, a silhouette between the trees, fur so dark it was almost black. It was perfectly still, head upright, ears cocked, listening for them. Gawain snapped his head back behind the cover of the ancient tree. Had it seen him? He guessed not, otherwise that monster would have been upon them already. But it was close. *Too* close. It would have their scent in moments.

Floundering for a way out of the situation, Gawain was struck by sudden inspiration. He reached past Robert and pulled open his friend's satchel, reaching into it with both hands.

"What are you doing?" Robert whispered.

"Hush," warned Gawain. He pulled the glazed ham from the pack and clutched the heavy lump of meat before him.

"When I signal, head for those trees," he said, gesturing with his head. Robert nodded in understanding.

Gawain poked his head around the trunk again, his breathing ragged, and rapidly blinking the sweat from his eyes. The beast had its back to him this time, though it was closer. Much closer. With all his might, Gawain hurled the ham across the clearing. It arced over the creature's head and crashed into the bushes opposite, making a heavy thud as it landed. As soon as the beast lumbered after it, Gawain took off, sprinting away from the ferocious animal with Robert trailing after him.

When he could run no further, calves like jelly, lungs burning, Gawain collapsed to the mulch of leaf pulp and composted foliage. His friend dropped beside him, wheezing, and rasping.

"What. Was. That. Thing?" panted Robert. He was on all fours, sweat dripping from his face and pattering onto the brown mulch.

"Bear," gulped Gawain, prostrate, spreadeagled on his back, as though preparing to make dirt-angels in the thick, fuzzy slurry that carpeted the forest floor. "Big one. Brown bear. Must have. Been hungry."

"Why didn't. It make. Noise?" asked Robert, rolling onto his back.

Gawain shuddered at the memory of the huge animal rearing up on its hind legs, forepaws spread wide, displaying its terrible claws, and its jaws, a gaping maw filled with hideous, sabre-like canines — each the length of a man's finger — designed for ripping flesh from bone. Worst of all was the complete absence of sound. The dreadful creature did not roar as Gawain expected. Instead, it loomed over them like silent death, waiting to pounce and tear them limb from limb. He shook the memory loose, lest it paralyse him again, and sat up, brushing the bits of dried fern and desiccated leaf from his sleeves.

"I was looking forward to that ham," moaned Robert, snapping each word with teenage petulance.

"I was doing you a favour," chuckled Gawain, patting his friend's belly. "Plus, it was starting to smell. Although that might be you. Come on."

Gawain jumped to his feet and set off again, heading towards the orange glow that he could just make out through the thick tree canopy.

"Hey! Wait up!" called Robert, clambering to his feet, and chasing after Gawain. He soon caught up but had to jog to keep pace with his taller friend. Sunset was nearing at the end of their first day, and Gawain did not want to bed down in the forest — he was keen to get beyond the perilous environment, with wild animals potentially lurking in every shadow, behind every tree. And at night, the real predators would come out. There was no rest to be had here and walking in this environment in the dark was a twisted ankle waiting to happen.

They slept in shifts that first night, whilst the other tended the fire in the small gully at the mountain's base and kept watch for any curious beasts that strayed too close. Too exhausted to eat, Gawain had passed out in seconds, grateful for Robert's offer to take first watch. Two hours passed in mere moments and then it was his turn to stand guard. This time, his stomach rumbled, so he tucked into his meagre rations of cheese, bread, and fruit. Gawain had not properly thought this through – this was certainly not enough food to see him safely to his destination and back again. Perhaps Robert's judicious stash of provisions was not so ridiculous after all?

They moved on at first light, and soon located the rock configuration and twisted oak, marked on his grandfather's map, that indicated the correct path up the mountainside. They made the steady climb up the mountain's least steep slope, heading for the pass — the path that cut through the mountain range. The map led them through the most direct route to the unsettled wildlands beyond. It was treacherous and narrow in places, certainly nothing like the trade route used by merchants a few miles south of this one, though it was certainly the quickest way to reach the valley. According to the map, that was where they must go.

At least there were no dangerous beasts up here, Gawain reflected, as he edged across a ledge where the narrow pathway had crumbled, leaving a gap several feet across. He and Robert were linked at the waist by a length of rope, should one of them lose their footing, though Gawain feared that would likely drag them both from their perch and send them plummeting towards the jagged rocks a hundred feet below. Mountain goats watched the nervous travellers with something akin to amusement, gambolling above them, leaping from rock to rock, seemingly oblivious to the certain death that lay below.

Aside from the terrain, their second day was uneventful, though arduous. Though, when they reached the rickety rope and wooden-slat bridge that connected two mountains about a third of the way along the pass, Gawain did fear he would have to travel the rest of the way alone. Robert simply refused to set foot on the bridge, fearing it would not hold his weight. An hour of gentle cajoling and coaxing that descended into bullying and name-calling seemingly did nothing to affect his friend's resolve.

"Please," Gawain pleaded. "I can't go on without you, Bobby. I'll carry your bag and I'll go behind you every step of the way. If you fall, I fall."

Robert finally relented and handed his bag to Gawain. He stepped to the edge of the precipice, placed one tremulous foot on the first creaking plank and, gripping the rough rope rails as though his life depended on it, he stepped out onto the bridge. The crossing was slow and terrifying, the expanse seeming much broader than it actually was. They survived the ordeal, almost crawling onto the granite apron that awaited them on the other side. They lay there, panting, gulping down sweet air as though they had run several miles.

"Well done, Bobby," said Gawain, patting his friend's quivering shoulder before helping him to his feet.

The third day was positively serene, as they followed the meandering stream that weaved through the verdant valley floor. For the first time since they left home, Robert seemed happy, and the pair exchanged jokes, telling stories, munching on apples and dried apricots as they trudged through the long grass.

The waterfalls provided a beautiful backdrop, and a welcome opportunity to douse themselves in cool water to counter the scorching midday sun. By the time they reached the seventh and final fall, the sun had begun to set, and so Gawain clambered up the grassy verge until he reached the top of the rise. And there, just as Grandfather Sanson had told him, was the fortress. It stood atop a forbidding, slate-grey peak, incongruous with the green surroundings, jutting out from the earth like a broken bone. At its apex stood the crumbling walls and buildings of the fortress – long derelict and without signs of life. Only the tower seemed untouched by time, rising tall and proud, a hundred feet above the collapsed ruins. The sky immediately above it roiled with heavy, rain-swollen clouds. The rock was less than a mile away, so they would easily reach it tomorrow morning. For now, it was time to make camp.

They clambered down the hill and made their fire in the green basin in the rock's elongated shadow, cast by the setting sun. The field was dotted with fragrant, red flowers, whilst the long grass was soft and comfortable for their aching muscles as they settled down, resting before the big day ahead.

***

Gawain woke with a start, his head muzzy, swimming, vision blurred. For a moment, his mind returned to a few nights before when he had shared some wine with his grandfather. He looked around, confused. The fire had gone out and Robert was fast asleep.

"Robert," he called, though his voice sounded strange to him. Slurred. As though his tongue was too big for his mouth. He tried to stand, but his legs would not support his weight and he slumped to the ground. What on earth was up with him? And then it hit him, like the pungent, sweet aroma all around, tickling his sinuses and scratching his throat. It was the flowers. They must get out of here!

Gawain dragged himself to Robert's slumbering form and shook him until he began to rouse.

"Gerroff," Robert mumbled in protest.

"Bobby! Wake up!" cried Gawain, violently shaking his friend. Terror had sparked his senses, and he was now wide awake. As he peered into the darkness, the horrified realisation that they were no longer alone prickled Gawain's senses. Darker shapes shuffled towards them, closing on every side, though the overcast night sky left little light for him to clearly make them out. Just then, as though reading his mind, the clouds parted, and the moon's pale blue light illuminated the scene. Gawain rather wished it had not.

Shambling towards them were a dozen mouldering corpses, held together by stringy, rotting sinews. Some of them had lost limbs, withered to nothingness, whilst others appeared relatively fresh, still muscular, their clothes intact. They all had one thing in common: they exuded hunger. And Gawain knew, deep in the pit of his terrified soul, what these ghouls were ravenous for.

He slapped Robert with all his strength, which did the trick.

"What?" Robert shrieked, clutching his cheek. "Why did you hit me?"

"Get up! Now!" ordered Gawain, in a tone that brooked no argument. He hauled Robert to his feet, then thrust one of the old swords into his hand.

"Oh, shit…" mumbled Robert, suddenly becoming aware of his surroundings. He almost dropped the sword.

"Come on," said Gawain. "Target the oldest-looking ones. Head for the tower."

Gawain launched himself at the most desiccated creature, slashing at it with all the force he could muster. The thing fell apart as his blade cut through it, its bones as brittle as a stale baguette. The things followed, reaching out with urgent fingers, desperately clutching at the boys, snapping their rotting jaws.

The pair inexpertly hacked and slashed their way clear of the undead mob, as more of the creatures closed in from all around. There must have been hundreds of them. The boys ran, the first rays of sunlight at their backs, heading for the rock. They reached its base, where steps had been carved into its side, and hurtled up them, fear giving their muscles strength. Several steps up the great natural monolith, Gawain turned back to check on his pursuers, but the dreadful horde had ceased their chase and had gathered around the rock's base.

Gawain gulped at the sight. Hundreds? Thousands of them at least, their eyes locked on the living intruders.

"What *are* they?" gasped Robert. "What do they want?"

"I don't know," shuddered Gawain. "I don't think I want to find out."

They rested, regathering their strength, though the audible rumble of their stomachs betrayed their hunger; they had left their food behind on the plain below. They did not even have their water skins to wet their parched tongues.

"Come on," groaned Gawain, reluctantly lifting himself off the uncomfortable stone steps.

The pair laboured their weary way up the winding, serpentine staircase without exchanging a word. Upwards was the only way. Down was not an option. About three-quarters of the way up, Gawain made the mistake of looking down at the plain below. There were more of the things gathered there now, surrounding the outcrop, filling the basin as far as the eye could see. He could feel their eyes on him and Robert, watching their every move.

"What are they?" asked Robert again, his teeth chattering, as much from hunger as from the cold, Gawain guessed. His own stomach growled as a reminder of its emptiness.

"I don't know," he admitted. "Grandfather never came this far. He never ventured beyond the valley of the falls."

"They look... dead," murmured Robert. "But not dead. Still moving."

"I know," snapped Gawain. He did not want to think about them. He could still see their milky eyes, their grasping, needful hands and snapping jaws each time he closed his eyes. Many of them had skin like dried meat, their clothes rotted to mere strips of rags. Others wore rusted armour and chainmail. More disturbingly, some were almost able to pass for living in the low light. Only the pallor of their skin and pale eyes gave them away. And they looked angry. As though furious with the living.

"My grandpa once told me about the dead who rise," said Robert. "Servants of evil, he called them. He said they feast on the flesh of the living. Mindless, like animals, spreading disease and destruction everywhere they go."

"Just stories," dismissed Gawain.

"Stories?" snorted Robert. "We were almost eaten by them! They're down there waiting for us. Thousands of them."

"I know, Bobby. I don't need you to remind me."

"How are we going to get back home? We have to go back down there at some point."

"I… I don't know," floundered Gawain. "I'll deal with that when I have to. For now, let's just focus on getting to the top and finding the princess."

Robert nodded, reluctantly, and trudged behind his companion and best friend in silence for a way.

"Why haven't they followed us?" Robert asked after a while.

"I don't know, Bobby."

"It's like they're afraid."

"Bobby, please."

"What could those monsters possibly be scared of?"

"Bobby! Shut up!"

They completed their climb in sullen silence, finally arriving, exhausted, at the apron before the outer gate. The sun was high in the sky, though the air remained chilly at this altitude, and Gawain's shirt clung to his back, plastered to his skin with sweat.

The gatehouse's huge wooden doors were splintered ruins, their dry remains hanging from bent and broken hinges. The barbican still stood, though much of the circular perimeter wall that ringed the complex had crumbled and collapsed into the bailey, along with most of the watchtowers. The inner keep was in much the same condition, and its gate lay wide open, the portcullis a rusted, deformed lattice of iron, permanently wedged into the gateway jamb. Few of the interior buildings remained intact, weathered by the elements and time itself, with creeping vines smothering the piles of rubble. However, the tower and the collection of adjoined buildings at its base were a completely different story. They appeared as though construction had been completed just days ago, seemingly untouched by time. Their stonework looked pristine, whilst the mortar appeared fresh. The tower itself was imposing, with not a break in its curved surface until the row of windows near its distant apex. Its roof was pointed, clad in reddish/brown slates, with ornamental crenelations around the rim to capture rainfall and propel it away from the building's walls. Gawain had seen similarly impressive buildings on his infrequent trips to the larger neighbouring towns with his father and grandfather, but this one shared none of the hallmarks of an old building, not even staining from the weather or bird faeces.

"What happened to this place?" whispered Robert.

"Time," replied Gawain, hefting his sword. "Come on."

Gawain proceeded towards the main structure, creeping across the bailey's packed earth. He clutched the door's loop handle and twisted it. It moved with barely a sound, and the door swung smoothly inwards into a small, well-lit antechamber.

"Come on," mouthed Gawain, beckoning to Robert. His friend looked petrified, and hesitated at the doorway, seemingly unwilling to follow. But Gawain knew Robert would not leave him alone, and he soon screwed up his courage and stepped over the threshold. They followed the narrow corridor, lit by torches mounted in wall sconces, until it opened out into another, much larger chamber. On the other side, stood a door. The door to the tower.

It was not the door that first grabbed Gawain's attention. Before it, laid out on low pedestals, were seven figures, each clutching a weapon — some wielding swords, others an axe, and one with a spiked iron mace — clenched between thick, gnarled fingers and laid across their body. Each armoured figure had a shaggy beard beneath gruff features, and an iron helmet keeping their thick, wiry hair in check. Each was shorter than a man, yet thick shouldered and muscular. They were not dead, yet not alive either. It was as though they were... stuck... suspended in a state of changelessness. Waiting. For what, Gawain did not know.

"Who are they?" gasped Robert.

"The dwarves,"

"The what now?"

"Have you not heard of the dwarves?" whispered Gawain. "You must know the story, Bobby? Seven dwarven warriors of great renown – the finest soldiers in all the land. They wait here to protect the princess lest the evil queen return to finish her off. My grandmother told me the queen could never rest whilst the princess lived, even if there was just a small chance that the curse would be broken. And so, the dwarves remained as her protectors. Oh, the wicked queen sent hundreds of would-be assassins against them, but the dwarves prevailed each time. Only the worthy may pass."

"My mum never said nothing about no dwarves," Robert insisted. "She said seven great and powerful *knights* stood watch over her, warding off evil."

"Same thing," growled Gawain. "Nobody said the knights had to be tall, Bobby. You can see them with your own eyes!"

"Okay, okay," Robert conceded. "Just one thing though?"

"Yes?"

"How are these dwarves – knights, or whatever they are – supposed to determine who is worthy and who isn't?"

"What d'you mean?"

"I mean – I'm just saying – wouldn't it make more sense for them to chase off *anyone* who came near? Who's got time to listen to a load of would-be suitors wanting to make off with their princess? After all this time, I'm guessing they're a bit protective."

"I… um… well," stammered Gawain. "Actually, you've got a point."

Gawain scratched his jaw for a moment, then brushed his matted, grubby hair back from his temples as he contemplated the next step. He had come too far to turn back now. Besides, he had no desire to go back down into the plain until those horrible creatures had dispersed.

And then, it struck him.

"I have an idea," he beamed.

"No! No way! Not a chance!" said Robert.

"Sssssshhh," hissed Gawain. "You'll wake them! Besides, what are you so afraid of, Bobby? They're old. You're taller, younger, faster. They'll never catch you."

"What am I afraid of?" gasped Robert, his voice rising an octave in incredulity. "Um, how about that bugger and his massive axe? I wouldn't be much taller than him for long if he got his hands on me."

"Ah, you're worried he'll cut off your head?"

"Well. I was thinking he'd cut my legs off at the knee, but thanks for that."

"Listen, listen," soothed Gawain. "I just need you to buy me a few seconds. Just lead them away from the door so I can slip past and head up into the tower. Ten seconds at most. Once they think they've scared you off, they'll give up the chase."

"And how do you get past them on the way down?"

"Easy. I'll have the princess with me, woken from the curse, and they'll have no reason to attack. It will work. I promise."

"You promise?" said Robert, Gawain nodded, grinning, exuding that ready confidence that came to him so effortlessly. "Oh, alright then."

"Good man!" said Gawain. "And when I'm king, I'll make you my chief knight of whatever. Deal?"

Before Robert could respond, Gawain shoved him into the room then ducked back out of view.

Robert stepped cautiously into the chamber, looking for any sign of movement from the prone guards.

"Hello?" he tried, timidly. There was no response.

On the ground, near his foot was a round shield — a simple affair, beaten from a sheet of what appeared to be bronze, then reinforced with a wooden frame, fastened to the metal with rounded lug bolts. He slipped his left hand through the leather straps and held it protectively before him. He glanced back to the corridor, where Gawain had poked his head out and was nodding, encouragingly. Robert faced front, took a deep breath, then repeatedly pounded his sword against the shield. The metallic clanging rang around the chamber, echoing off the walls and ceiling. The effect was instantaneous. All seven dwarves sat bolt upright, staring at the intruder with murder in their eyes. The central dwarf – a head taller than the others, with braids in his beard – opened his mouth and released a guttural cry of rage. He held his sword aloft and pointed it at Robert. As one, the dwarves hopped down from their plinths and charged at him.

It took a moment for Robert to unfreeze, but he scampered for the corridor to his left with the dwarves in hot pursuit. As he left the chamber, Robert glanced behind, just in time to see Gawain dart across it and pass through the tower's door.

***

"More bloody steps," moaned Gawain as he paused for breath. He had no idea how far up the structure he had travelled, up these perfectly hewn steps. With no windows and no point of reference aside from the occasional burning sconce, he just had to have faith he would arrive at the top eventually.

He took a deep breath, then soldiered on.

***

Robert hid beside the doorway of the small room, trying his best to keep his breathing under control. Gawain had been right – Robert was much quicker than the dwarves in a flat race. Unfortunately, there were not too many straights within this structure for him to put much distance between himself and his pursuers. The place was a maze – one the dwarves surely knew much better than he. Instead, all he could do was hide. He never stayed in one place for too long and, fortunately, the dwarven knights were not particularly stealthy, so he was able to hear them coming long before they were anywhere near him.

Robert desperately needed to retrace his steps and find his way back outside. One of these doorways must lead out there, surely?

As the sound of clomping footsteps died away, Robert slipped back into the corridor, made a left, then a right, then another left, where he found himself in the long hallway that led back to the main chamber. He dashed for it, abandoning his attempts to soft-shoe, almost able to taste freedom's cool, crisp air.

He heard the gruff bellow behind him, soon joined by a melee of angry voices. He had no time to turn back – he was almost there, almost fr—

Robert's leg's folded beneath him before he even felt the heavy spar collide with the back of his knees. He sprawled across the stone floor, skidding to a painful halt inside the main chamber. A large, double-headed battle-axe skittered to a half beside him, and he quickly rolled onto his back and clutched at his lower limbs, realising, with no little relief, that they were still attached.

Within seconds, the axe-thrower was upon him, gripping him by the collar and shaking him, roughly.

"Don't panic, boy," he snarled. "If I meant to cleave off your legs, I would have done."

"Let him go, Grincheux," said the tallest dwarf.

"Aye, Chief," said the axe-thrower. He pulled Robert's face close to his, curled his lip into a snarl before releasing him with obvious reluctance.

"Please don't kill me!" begged Robert, his arms held out, protectively.

"Kill you?" chuckled the lead dwarf. "Why would we kill you? We try not to kill anyone, lad. You not seen what happens to them that dies around here? I wouldn't wish that even on me mother-in-law. No, we just chase off the likes o' you where we can. Less trouble all 'round. Though there are more o' them buggers down below all the time."

"What are they?" asked Robert.

"Buggered if I know," said the lead dwarf, crouching beside Robert. "They started turning up not long after we arrived here. Anyone dies 'round here, they turn into one o' them bastards. Turned a few of 'em meself, 'til we figured out what were goin' on."

"Right, okay, but why won't they come up here?"

"Scared," declared the dwarf.

"What? Of you?"

"The seven of us?" scoffed the dwarf. "Don't be bloody daft, lad!"

"Who are you?" asked Robert, as the dwarf helped him up.

"My name is Perceval – Percy to my friends – and I have the dubious pleasure of leading this bunch of reprobates. We are the guardians of the tower." Robert looked at the crowd of dwarven warriors crowded around him. They were more amused than angry, it seemed. Except for Grincheux.

"Hello…" said Robert, weakly.

"Now, what's a pudgy little fella like you doing sneaking around here?" asked Percy. "Thought you'd come seeking your fortune, eh? Well, the bad news is, you're out of luck, lad. Nothing here worth nickin', as I'm sure you can see. Unless yer trying to collect a bunch of crusty old soldiers, that is." The dwarves dutifully chuckled.

"No, nothing like that, sir," insisted Robert. "I'm no thief. We just… I mean… that is to say—"

"We?" said Percy, his eyes narrowed. "You not alone, lad?"

"I… we don't mean any harm, sir. We have no malicious intent. Gawain believes he is worthy—"

"Worthy?" Percy stood bolt upright, then gestured to the one called Grincheux. The cantankerous dwarf gathered up his axe and ran to the tower's door. He gripped the handle and rattled it but, try as he might, it would not budge. Grincheux turned to Percy and shook his head, gravely.

"Oh bugger," groaned Percy. "What have you gone and done, lad?"

***

Gawain finally reached the top of the stairwell, arriving at a narrow landing before a pale, varnished wooden door. It was just like the one in his dream, though he had no time to dwell on that. He leant against the wall, bent double and threw up, hurling disgusting green bile as there was nothing else left to come up. He wiped his mouth and spat, in a vain attempt to rid his mouth of the foul taste.

He had come too far to let his exhausted body stop him now.

Gawain staggered forward, gripped the knob and, steadying himself against the frame, pushed at the door. It glided open without effort or sound.

Inside, lying on a stone slab, was the most beautiful woman Gawain had ever seen: her skin, pale and blemish-free, her lips the deep red of ripened cherries, and her hair, raven black, cascading in perfect ringlets that framed her high-cheeked, heart-shaped face.

To Gawain, she was perfect.

***

"What's going on?" cried Robert, as three of the dwarves attempted to pry the tower's entry open with an axe wedged between the door and the frame.

"Idiot boys!" grumbled Grincheux.

"Gawain just wants to free the princess," protested Robert. "To release her from her curse. He dreamt about her. He wants to help her. You don't need to protect her from him."

"She's bloody getting stronger," Grincheux snarled. "Reaching out."

"You don't understand, lad," chided Percy. "We're not 'ere to protect 'er from the likes o' you. We're here to protect every other bugger from 'er!"

***

Gawain, staggered into the room, edging closer to her, marvelling at her beauty. His heart was aflutter, hands trembling as he sat down on the slab and gazed upon the princess.

She was magnificent! She did not look much older than Gawain himself, though she radiated an indefinable age.

He felt... *drawn* to her. It was as though she glowed from inside.

Gawain leaned forward, edging closer, and kissed her ruby lips.

The princess's eyes snapped open. They were black. Not the black of night, nor the black of coal. They were much darker than that.

Gawain gasped and pulled away.

The princess's lips broke into a beatific smile. Then she sat up. She surveyed Gawain, head tilted to one side, staring lovingly upon him. She raised a hand, stroked his cheek and he could feel the gratitude emitting from her. Then she leaned in and kissed him again. Deeper, more passionately this time.

To Gawain, the kiss seemed to last for eternity.

Certainly, it lasted for the rest of his life.

***

Robert followed Percy and the dwarf warriors out into the courtyard, beyond the gate and to the top of the rock's steps. They looked down onto the plain below, as the army of the undead poured forth. The ground rumbled beneath their feet as thousands of mouldering, animated corpses thundered up the steps towards them.

"What's happening?" cried Robert.

"You have any kind of God in you, lad?" asked Percy.

"What? Well, I mean… I go to church sometimes."

"Well, you best start praying hard, lad. They're coming."

"What for?" pleaded Robert.

"Their queen," growled Grincheux. "Some dickhead has only gone and woke her up."

***

Gawain stared down at his lifeless body, slumped to the floor, arm twisted unnaturally behind his back.

He called out to the princess as she swayed past him, his sword in her hand, as though he were not there. He reached out to her, but his fingers passed through her arm. She did not respond, seemingly oblivious to his presence. She just pulled open the door and began to descend the stairs.

"Do not worry," said a warm, deep voice. "The worst is over. For you, at least."

Gawain turned towards his strange new companion – tall, clad all in black robes as dark as the princess's eyes.

"Who… who are you?" Gawain asked. He felt as though he should be afraid, yet he felt no fear. He felt… nothing.

"I am a friend," said the figure. "Here to guide you on your journey."

Gawain paused. "I… I think my grandfather told me about you. Are you…?"

"Yes."

"Then I'm...?"

"I am afraid so?"

"Huh..."

Gawain had expected a little more than this. He thought there would be pain. Or grief. *Something.* Instead, he felt... at peace. He looked down at his former body as it twitched, then jerked, before slowly clambering back to his former feet. It turned to face him, and his former eyes were washed-out and grey, though he was otherwise just as Gawain remembered himself.

"Um... are you sure I'm dead?" he asked.

"Yes," said the stranger. "Unfortunately for you, the lights are on, but whatever is at home is not you."

Gawain watched as his former self staggered through the door and followed the princess down the steps.

"So, what now?" he asked.

The stranger placed a comforting arm around Gawain's metaphorical shoulders.

"That, my young friend," he said, "is entirely up to you."

Hoard

AD 529, Llanteulyddog, the Kingdom of Dyfed, Albion.

Sir Gildas Boldhart dismounted his horse and tied her up at the hitching post outside the Farrier's Arms Inn. He removed his shiny helmet, smoothed down his crisply trimmed, light brown hair and, with a world-weary sigh, entered the establishment.

Inside, the atmosphere was rambunctious and lively, more so than the knight would have expected for a midweek afternoon, but who knew how these savages lived in such rural backwaters?

Rumour had it the king was from somewhere near here, not that Gildas had spoken to his monarch – not for some time. Not since *the incident*. He was certain Arthur had sent him here to get him out of the way. Gildas hated leaving Camelot, let alone the Kingdom of Logres, but since losing his seat at the king's high table, the disgraced knight had found his assignments taking him further and further afield. And now here? To the arse-end of nowhere, chasing a bloody cattle thief and rural pest, pursuing a creature no one had seen in centuries.

A dragon, indeed! The very idea made Gildas's blood boil.

"Ah, prynhawn da. You must be Sir Boldhart?"

Gildas turned to face the speaker, a jolly, plump little man with a thick beard. He rose from his table, dabbing his mouth with a napkin. The man hurried over to him, taking his hand and shaking it, enthusiastically.

"Welcome to Llanteulyddog," said the man, his voice bright and musical. "First time in Dyfed?"

"Yes, indeed," said Gildas, with far less enthusiasm. "You must be—"

"Dafydd Griffiths," interrupted the man. "I'm the mayor, so I have the dubious pleasure of being the main man in these parts – overseeing the runnin' of the town council, administration, enforcing the law and what have hyou."

"I see—"

"And a big part o' that is dealing with complaints from my constituents, see?"

"And they're complaining about a dragon, right?" said Gildas, his expression impassive, though his single raised eyebrow was as effusive as any sneer.

"Shush now," grumbled the mayor. "We don't use the 'D' word in these parts. Causes panic now, innit? Come with me."

Griffiths led Gildas to a table at the back of the room, where a small group of men were gathered around two pulled-together tables, leaning in, and talking in hushed, conspiratorial tones. They all had the bearing, weathered skin, and terse demeanour of working men – farmers, Gildas presumed.

"Now then," said Griffiths, clapping his hands together. "These fine fellows are from our civic council, representing our agricultural industry: Hywel Wogan, Ifor Meredith, Morfan Bach, Tegwyn Jenkin, and Ithel Dew."

Farmers, thought Gildas, fighting to keep the mental sneer from showing in his expression. Just as he suspected. He knew men like this. They tended towards realism and did not hold with nonsense and fairy tales. The day was looking up.

"And this," continued Griffiths, gesturing a meaty paw in Gildas's direction, "is Sir Gildas Boldhart of the court of

King Arthur Pendragon, sent here as a special favour to King Vortiporius, to help us with our – ahem – *problem*."

"You mean the dragon?" said the one called Hywel, folding his arms and sitting back, his expression grim.

"Shush, Hywel," hissed Griffiths. "You know what it's like round hyur when a rumour gets started. There'll be panic! The bloody magistrate'll have me guts for garters."

"I don't hold wi' that nonsense, as it 'appens," said Ithel, easily the oldest of the farmers. "Reckon its bloody kids, muckin' about or summat."

"Most likely the bloody Irish," spat Tegwyn. "Can't be trusted, them lot."

Gildas smiled and pulled up a chair. He liked men like this – they were much more *his* kind of people: pragmatists, believing only the things they could see with their eyes and feel with their hands.

"So, where have these rumours of mythical beasts come from?" the knight asked. The farmers exchanged dark glances, though none put a voice to their thoughts. "There must be a reason?"

The old men reached an unspoken agreement.

Hoard

"Right then," said Hywel. "We'd better show you."

The overcast sky drained all warmth from the late afternoon, bringing with it the promise of rain, though the breeze was mercifully mild up in the hills today. Gildas crouched beside the area of scorched ground and touched it, tentatively. For some reason, he expected it to be warm and was slightly disappointed that it was not. He inspected the patina of black soot coating his fingertips.

"This was yesterday," Hywel explained. "Been happening every few days for a couple of months, see?"

Gildas had seen many inexplicable things in his time serving Arthur — particularly wherever the royal advisor, Merlin, was involved — but he had never seen anything like this. A circle, around ten feet across had been charred to a blackened disc. Nearest to the centre, the earth and rock had melted into something resembling glass. And at the very heart of the charred patch, the seared remains of a body, the rib cage poking at the sky like black fingers. Much of the carcass had been vaporised.

"What was it?" The knight asked.

"A sheep," Tegwyn told him. "One o' my lot."

"It's not always sheep, though," added Ifor. "I lost a couple o' pigs, a cow, and even a horse."

"Always the same as this?" asked Gildas. "And nobody has seen anything?"

"Always the same," replied Hywel. "And always at night. I saw a flash of light on my property last week. By the time I got there, I found the same as this: one o' my cows burned to a crisp. Nothin' left but a circle o' burnt grass."

Gildas nodded, casting his eyes across the hilly landscape beneath the blanket of endless cloud. It had taken them an hour to trek out here. Besides the farm, there were no other residences for miles.

"Where did the suggestion of dragons come from?" he asked.

"That'd be my good lady, Missus Bach," said Morfan, his cheeks flushing as the other farmers glared at him. "She believes in all that stuff."

"You need to tell her to keep her yap shut," growled Hywel.

"Myfanwy?" chuckled Morfan. "You're welcome to tell yourself, Hywel. See what that gets you, apart from a permanent limp." The other men grinned and looked away. Myfanwy Bach was a formidable woman – one none of them fancied running afoul of.

Mayor Griffiths explained how Missus Bach had rallied the other farmer's wives around and approached him directly, demanding he did something to tackle the "dragon pest".

"And you took them seriously?" smiled Gildas.

"Listen, young fellow-me-lad," said Griffith. "You ne'er been on the wrong side o' a tongue-lashing from Myfanwy Bach, 'a'hyou? That bloody battle-axe is not someone you want to ignore, innit? No offence, Morfan."

"None taken," shrugged Bach, with an expression that declared he knew how it felt to be on the wrong end of his wife's temper better than anyone.

"And why are you so sure it isn't a dragon?" asked the knight.

"Stands to reason, innit?" declared Hywel. "There's no such bloody thing."

Gildas grinned. "I see. Then why do you need me?"

"Well, that's the thing, as it 'appens," mumbled the mayor. "What if we're wrong, see? I mean, we all heard the stories o' King Arthur's adventures. If it is a dragon, who better to get rid of it than one o' the famous knights of the Round Table?"

Gildas snorted, shaking his head. Yes, he knew the stories, carried far and wide by bards, usually on the orders of Merlin. They told of dragons, trolls, mermaids, and ghastly spectres – any number of strange and impossible beasts. Gildas had to admit, Arthur was a formidable warrior, though he had never seen his king take on anything more unusual than a very tall Saxon soldier that many had revered as a giant. He had been freakishly big, for sure, but he was just a man. Arthur had certainly cut him down to size. This was something different. It felt… strange.

"You e'er seen summat do this kind o' damage afor?" asked Griffiths.

"No, never," said Gildas. He had seen all sorts of weapons in his campaigns with Arthur, including fearsome trebuchets, able to hurl great, burning barrels of pitch huge distances, igniting their targets, be they men, horses, buildings. And still, they did not cause this kind of focussed, concentrated devastation. Nothing he knew of could generate this kind of heat – not even Merlin and his magical wildfire.

"So, any ideas?" asked Hywel. "You must have some thoughts on who or what could be behind this?"

"No, not yet," replied Gildas. "But I *will* find out."

***

Gildas relaxed, leaning back in his chair, and rubbing his full stomach. He was pleasantly surprised by the food at the Farrier's Arms, and he had polished off a plate of salted pork, served with potatoes, cabbage and leek, finished with a thick slice of buttered bara brith, crammed with dried fruit.

"All to your liking, sir?" asked Gwen, the innkeeper's wife.

"Delicious, thank you," smiled Gildas. "My compliments – especially for your delicious fruit bread."

"Ah, thank you, sir. The bara brith is an old family recipe. My mother taught me when I was a girl and I'll teach it to my daughter when the time is right."

Hoard

Gildas took a swig of his ale as the innkeeper cleared the table and he sighed, contentedly. Perhaps this assignment was not so bad after all. It had been some time since he had enjoyed such pleasant surroundings and been able to relax. Even the simple pleasure of a sit-down meal was a distant memory. Mealtimes in Arthur's palace could be fractious occasions, especially in the politically charged world of the king's court. Knights were ambitious, vying for position amongst their ranks, desperate to capture the king's attention – something Arthur actively encouraged. Since his expulsion from the Round Table, Gildas was viewed as a lame duck, so it was nice not to walk into a room and hear a sudden silence, accompanied by sideways glances and hostile sneers. Even as an outsider, the locals here hardly gave him a moment's notice.

The sound of a genteelly cleared throat roused the knight from his reverie, and he looked around to see a man standing next to his table. He was tall, with the square-shouldered bearing of a soldier – not like one of the locals at all. He wore a brown leather jerkin, with a darker undershirt, plumb leather britches, and knee-high black riding boots. None of the clothes matched, but they were all of high quality, if somewhat aged. From his thick, black sword-belt, hung a knightly sword, its decorative pommel cast in the shape of a lion, inlaid with gold plate. And yet, Gildas was certain this man was no knight.

"May I join you?" asked the man, taking the seat opposite without waiting for a response.

"Do I have a choice?"

The man thrust out his hand. "Osmund Hereweald," he said. "Pleased to meet you, sir."

Gildas tentatively shook the man's hand. "Gildas Boldhart."

"Oh, I know who you are, Sir Boldhart."

"Have we met?"

"Met? No, though we have shared a battlefield more than once."

"On the same side?" asked Gildas.

The man grinned. "On occasion, certainly."

Just as Gildas suspected. This man was a mercenary – a soldier of fortune, willing to fight for the highest bidder. Gildas distrusted such men, though he did see their value in times of war, as long as your enemy did not pay them to switch sides, that is.

"What can I do for you, Mister Hereweald?"

"Osmund, please," grinned the mercenary. "And it is more a case of what *I* can do for *you*."

"I'm listening."

"Okay," said Hereweald. "It seems to me you have something of a challenging assignment here."

"What do you know of it?" asked Gildas, sipping his ale, maintaining an implacable expression.

"I know you seek a dragon."

Gildas nodded thoughtfully, swilling the full-bodied beer around his mouth.

"Some would say there are no such creatures," he said, after a moment's silence.

"True," admitted Hereweald. "But as a man who has travelled this world in the service of many, many commanders, I have seen more things that should not exist than have any right to. Consequently, my mind is as open as a whore's legs."

Gildas had to admit, he too had seen many things his logical mind was unable to explain in his years of service to the crown. And, for Merlin, the impossible was his stock-in-trade. Gildas, however, preferred to trust his eyes and ears.

"And why do I need your help, Mister Hereweald?"

"Please, call me Osmund. And, to answer your question, I know how to locate your felon, be they dragon or otherwise."

Gildas sat forward, scanning the man for any signs of deceit, but all he saw was Hereweald's disarming grin. In truth, the knight had no idea where to start looking for this dragon or whatever it was. He had had Griffiths compile a list of all the known incidents, including dates and locations. Aside from the fact that the offender never struck in the same place in succession, there was no obvious pattern to speak of. Perhaps this newcomer could be of some help?

"So, what's your idea, Osmund?"

"Ah, now that would be telling," replied Hereweald, his grin broadening. "Not until we have an accord."

"Okay," nodded Gildas. "So, what do you want?"

"Not much," shrugged the mercenary. "If I prove of use to you, perhaps a good word in the right ear? I am always on the lookout for opportunities, and I am starting to think that a more permanent position might be favourable."

"If you know who I am, you surely know my word carries little value in King Arthur's court right now?"

"True," conceded Hereweald. "I have faith that this is nought but a momentary blip in your otherwise stellar career, Sir Boldhart – and it never hurts a man of my profession to establish friendships with those in high places. And I do have a secondary condition."

"I see. And that is?"

"If our perpetrator does prove to be a dragon, I want its hoard."

"Its hoard?" Gildas raised an amused eyebrow.

"Yes, its hoard," pressed Hereweald. "Everyone knows dragons sleep on a hoard of gold and precious treasures. If we find this dragon, I take its hoard. Do we have an agreement?"

Gildas considered the man's proposal for a moment, then reached out and shook his proffered hand.

***

In truth, Hereweald's plan was fiendish in its simplicity. So much so, that Gildas kicked himself for not thinking of it first.

"The problem is," Hereweald had reasoned, "you're trying to cover a spread of five farms, each of them with acres of land, each with several herds of cattle. Now, at this time of year, farmers tend to leave the cattle out in the fields at night, unless the weather turns, of course, except for morning and evening milking of the cows. So, what if we instruct the farmers to bring their cattle in – all except one – until we find the culprit? And if that farmer pens his herd within a single field, it narrows our search down to just one location."

Gildas had to admit, there was elegance in the plan's unsophistication. Hereweald clearly had a sharp, tactical mind.

After some negotiation, Hywell had volunteered his herd of sheep to remain outside. When asked why the farmers had not thought to bring in the creatures before, Hywel had reasoned, "We had no reason, innit? It's more hassle than its worth – there's no such bloody thing as dragons."

After two nights sat in a cold, damp field, surrounded by the pungent aroma of sheep shit, Gildas was inclined to agree. It was not one of those stenches you got used to, either. It seeped into your sinus, settled onto your clothes and skin until you felt like you would never wash the scent away, no matter how hard you scrubbed.

The sheep themselves kept their distance from where the pair of soldiers, had hunkered beneath a sycamore tree. The pair shared a flask of wine and picked at the cheese, ham, and bread that Gwen had packed for them. She had even sent a couple of large slabs of the delicious bara brith.

"So, tell me something, Sir Boldhart," asked Hereweald. "I heard you and the king had something of a disagreement? A parting of ways? Is that true?"

"Something like that," frowned Gildas. The knight still did not trust the mercenary but, after a couple of days together, he found him quite pleasant company.

"Come on! You can tell me," urged Hereweald. "What did you do?"

"I didn't do anything, Osmund," sighed Gildas.

"Was it Guinevere?" leered the mercenary. "I've heard she's no better than she should be. There's a few of your lot got in trouble with the king for that, so I hear."

"No, I didn't do anything like that."

"Then what did you do?"

"I was born, if you must know," snapped Gildas.

"What?"

"Earlier this year my mother, Lady Morgause, sadly passed away at her home in Lothian. Her illness was sudden but, before she passed, she wrote three letters: one to me, one to her husband, King Lot, and the third to Arthur. According to the letter, Arthur forced himself upon my mother some years ago, whilst she was newly married to the Lothian king and on a diplomatic visit to Camelot. I was the fruit of that union. When Lot found out, he was furious. He renounced me as his son and threatened war with Camelot. Arthur immediately removed me from the Round Table and has not spoken with me since. I have requested his council many times, but he will not see me."

"I'm sorry to hear that, my friend," said Hereweald. To Gildas' surprise, the mercenary seemed genuine. "I find, at times of strife, 'tis better to get royally pissed and forget about it until another day."

He handed the wineskin to Gildas. The knight smiled and took it, swigging from it, deeply, then handed it back to his companion.

"To... your mother," toasted Hereweald, holding the wine aloft. "May her place in the hereafter be filled with wines as good as this."

As the sun began to crest the horizon, the sky faded from black to a bruised purple and blue, streaked with oranges and yellows. Gildas sighed and rubbed his tired eyes.

"Well, that's another night without a sighting," he yawned. "I'm guessing our pranksters have heard we're around and are keeping their distance."

As Gildas rose to his feet and brushed the grass and dirt from his britches, Hereweald gripped the knight's forearm and, eyes wide in alarm, pointed across the field. Gildas looked, though could not immediately see what had caught the mercenary's attention. And then, like an optical illusion, suddenly he could see nothing else. Soaring through the darkness, gliding like an enormous swallow, swooped something big. No. Something huge! Nothing of such immense proportions had any right to fly. Its wings must have spanned twenty feet across, whilst its body was the size of a shire horse. Its long neck craned and focused on the panicked sheep, as they bleated and scattered in every direction, sensing the enormous predator above, as its long, armoured tail whipped back and forth, like an impatient cat ready to pounce. It circled the field in a wide parabola, completing several circuits before it settled on a target. It descended upon a single sheep, separated from its brethren and seemingly frozen in terror. The dragon hovered there, great wings beating, pummelling the air. It inhaled, its chest inflating like some great bellows, before unleashing a lance of blue-white flame so bright it scored itself onto the knight's retina. It went on for just a few seconds, though Gildas could still see it long after it ceased. He blinked, rubbing his eyes, only able to see purple and white blotches. By the time he refocused, the beast was on the ground, perched on its hindquarters, wings and tail splayed for balance, whilst its jaws clamped down on the sheep's charred remains, gorging itself on sizzling, blackened flesh.

"Come on," hissed Gildas, drawing his sword and heading towards the beast. Hereweald held him back.

"No! We should follow it. Back to its lair – its hoard! We agreed, remember?"

Gildas silently cursed the mercenary's greed but stayed his hand. An agreement was an agreement, and, like any knight, Gildas's word was his bond. Without honour, he had nothing.

*

"Keep up," called Hereweald, jogging across the field. The dragon was still in view in the dawn light, heading higher into the hills.

The beast had eaten its fill of charred meat in just a few minutes. Before taking flight, it had snapped its head around, staring at the two men, before leaping into the air once more.

They followed it over the hills for a couple of miles, just keeping the creature in sight, but they fell further back with every beat of the majestic creature's wings, and it would soon lose them.

In the insipid early daylight, they could see the dragon more clearly. Its armoured hide was an indefinable colour: pearlescent, appearing green in some lights, a deep red in others, and a strangely iridescent black in between. The leathery scales of its softer underbelly were a deep grey. It was, perhaps, the most beautiful creature Gildas had ever seen.

Just when the dragon seemed set to outdistance the pursuing soldiers, it banked hard to the right and alighted on the furthest hillside, near its apex. Then, it folded its wings, ducked its head, and entered a cave mouth which appeared far too small to accommodate such a massive beast.

"There!" cried Hereweald. "Its lair! We've found it."

It took almost an hour to trek the mile or so across the undulating landscape, the pair frequently losing their footing on the long, dew-soaked grass. They soon found their way to the cave's entrance. They stood there, catching their breath, in dread anticipation of what waited inside. From out here, Gildas could hear the gentle, rhythmic whoosh and snort of the dragon's breathing.

"What now?" asked the knight.

"Now, we go inside and claim our bounty," said Hereweald.

As the mercenary drew his sword and stepped towards the cave's maw, Gildas placed a hand on his companion's shoulder.

"Are you sure about this?" he asked.

"What?"

"It's just… we believed dragons extinct. Do we have a right to kill this one?"

"A right?" grinned Hereweald. "Gildas, men are masters of the world, my friend. The time of dragons has passed. If *we* do not kill the beast, someone else will."

"Where has it come from? After centuries, just to appear like this? Surely that must mean something?"

"Who cares?" snorted Hereweald. "You're thinking too deeply, Gildas. This thing is just an animal. Flesh and blood, nothing more. Right now, it's killing sheep and cows. And soon, if it gathers more strength, who's to say it won't start burning people? What if its next victim is a child, Sir Boldhart?"

"I understand your point, Osmund," argued Gildas. "But… it just doesn't *feel* right."

"Right?" said Hereweald. "Gildas, if we kill the dragon now, we'll be heroes. It may even be enough to earn a seat back at Arthur's table. Perhaps one for both of us? The famous dragon slayers! Bards will sing of our exploits for generations. Does *that* feel right?"

Gildas sighed and nodded reluctantly. Whilst Hereweald lit a small pile of kindling on the sheltered area of rock, the knight prepared a torch by wrapping the tip of a nearby fallen branch in pitch-soaked rags. He lit it with the small fire and the pair headed into the darkness.

Although the cave's mouth was just about big enough for the men to duck through, the cavity beyond opened out into a broad tunnel. They followed it for several yards, until they reached a large, hollow cavern, easily the size of a large human dwelling. And there, curled up in its centre, was the dragon, gently snoring. It looked so peaceful, sleeping off its recent meal.

Gildas cast the torch around the cavern and its walls glistened and twinkled as the quartz minerals caught the light. But there was no sign of anything more valuable – certainly nothing that could be described as a hoard. But the dragon's sleeping body was curled around something else. Rocks, perhaps? He took a step closer, his eyes adjusting to the dim orange light. And then realisation took hold. Despite their rough, stony appearance, the four identical ovoids were not rocks. They were eggs. Dragon eggs.

"What are you waiting for?" whispered Hereweald. "Kill the bloody thing!"

Gildas shook his head. "I… I don't think I can, Osmund. This dragon is protecting its young. There is no hoard here – just her clutch of eggs."

"No matter," growled Hereweald. "The eggs will serve as my compensation. I know a merchant who will pay me well for dragon eggs and any other parts of the beast I can salvage."

"You knew!" gasped Gildas. "You wanted the eggs all along, but you couldn't tackle the dragon yourself."

"Well, I wouldn't say I *knew*," grinned Hereweald. "I guessed as much. Now, are you going to hold strong to our accord or not?"

But then, something in the cave's ambiance subtly changed, and it took Gildas a moment to realise what it was. Not a new sound, more the absence of noise, as the dragon's soft, regular, slumbering breaths had ceased. And from the look in Hereweald's eyes, he had noticed it too. Both men turned their heads to see the dragon awake, its fearsome head looming over them, peering at them with something akin to interest.

And then it spoke.

Please, it said, *do not do this, Sir Gildas Boldhart.*

"How do you know my name?" the knight demanded. To his shock, the dragon's voice had arrived in his mind without first passing through his ears. Her tone was soft and melodic, though tinged with fear.

"Who are you talking to?" demanded Hereweald.

I can see your heart, the dragon told Gildas. *You are a good man — an honourable man. Not like this itinerant killer. Be wary of him, he has murder in his heart — and not just mine. He plans to take your life and steal my children. You must not let him. I implore you!*

Heart racing, Gildas turned towards Hereweald and knew the dragon spoke true.

"Gildas? What are you waiting for?" roared Hereweald. "Let's kill this beast before it kills us!"

The mercenary raised his sword and rushed at the dragon, though before he could clear the space between them, Gildas cut him down, his sword slicing through Hereweald's neck and shoulder, inflicting a gaping wound. The soldier collapsed to his knees, dropping his sword, and clutching at his neck. Blood seeped and pulsed through his fingers and gurgled from his lips as he stared, beseechingly at Gildas. There was nothing the knight could do for the man, even had he wanted to. As a man of honour, he was not given to allowing the suffering of others, and so, Gildas ran his blade through Hereweald's heart, ending his torment. The mercenary's body slumped to the ground, blood pooling on the cave floor and filling the enclosed space with the unmistakable, metallic tang that Gildas knew too well.

Thank you, Sir Boldhart, the dragon said. *You have done me a great service. My children and I are forever in your debt.*

"How did you know I would protect you?" he asked. "I have seen your power. You could have incinerated Osmund without my help."

That is true. Though I could not have flamed Hereweald without also killing you. And you do not deserve to meet your end like that - I had every faith that a good man such as you would come to our aid. Unlike men, my kind will not take the lives of the undeserving. We kill for sustenance and take no pleasure in it. I see greatness in you, Sir Boldhart. Unlike most of your kind, you live by your honour, even if you serve a king who has none. He is a murderer. A rapist. A vile stain on the world of men, corrupted by power and greed.

"How could you know this?" gasped Gildas. "Do you know King Arthur?"

I do not know him, but I know men. And I can see your heart, feel your thoughts, your emotions. I know the contents of your mother's letter, and you know what kind of a man your king — your true father — is. You know the truth of how you came into this world. And, as you know it, so do I.

Hoard

Gildas nodded, grimly. "I thank you for sparing my life," he said. "You must know you cannot remain here? I will not kill you, but others will come seeking you. Others like Hereweald."

You are right, said the dragon. *Soon my children will hatch and then my life's purpose will be fulfilled. I returned here from a distant land, returning to the place of my birth to deliver my clutch of eggs.*

"You will die?" asked Gildas, aghast.

That is the way of my kind, the dragon confirmed. *Be not distressed — I am at peace. And once my children are born, they will require a protector. That task would normally fall to my mate, but he was taken from me by vicious men on our journey home. When I am gone, they shall be defenceless. Will you be their guardian, Sir Boldhart?*

"Me?" gasped Gildas. "I don't know anything about taking care of children, let alone dragons."

Do not worry, said the dragon. *They just need fresh meat. They will soon learn to communicate with you — just as I am now — and tell you their needs. They will grow fast. And they will be loyal.*

"What do you mean?"

You suspect what fate awaits you if you should return to Camelot or Lothian, Sir Boldhart. You have a claim to both thrones and neither Pendragon nor Lot will allow you to live. You dream of seizing power — of taking control of your destiny.

Gildas' head sagged, his shoulders slumped. There was little point in denying the dragon's claims – she could see his very soul. She knew him as well as he knew himself.

I do not judge you, said the dragon. *You are more worthy than either man. Both thrones are your birthright.*

"How do you know this?" cried Gildas.

I know it because you know it, the dragon told him. *Even if you will not admit it to yourself. Imagine yourself at the head of an army, with my four children leading your forces. There are many others loyal to you — many who will support your claim. You will be unstoppable, Sir Boldhart.*

Hoard

For three more nights, Gildas sat with the dragon. She had no name, explaining that names were a human construct and dragons did not need monikers or titles. He even accompanied her on another hunt, this time tracking an unfortunate goat that strayed near to her lair. She was truly majestic.

On the fourth day, the eggs finally hatched, and four pale, feeble reptiles emerged. Their eyes were tightly shut, and their flimsy wings were still translucent as Gildas helped them from the remnants of the shell husks. They each clambered up his arms and nuzzled into his neck and hair.

And, with a final satisfied, grateful sigh, the dragon mother closed her eyes for the final time.

A week later, Sir Gildas Boldhart set off. He would head for Lothian, the place of his birth and the seat of power of the man he had always believed to be his father. The dragons were already much hardier. They could see now, and their armoured hide had begun to develop. They could even fly – if only for short distances – and they had already started to communicate with Gildas. Like their mother, they could see into their protector's mind. What was more, Gildas could feel their thoughts and emotions too. Not in the form of words – at least, not yet – though he understood their needs completely.

As a fine drizzle began to fall, the dragon whelps alternately fluttering above or riding on his shoulders or lap, Gildas plotted his next move. Spurring his horse into a trot, he headed north.

Arthur's knights would come in search of him, and so he abandoned the name given to him by the king of Camelot. He would no longer be known as Sir Gildas Boldhart. Instead, he would adopt his grandfather's name from his mother's side – perhaps the most feared knight in Christendom during his heyday.

From now on, he would be known as Mordred.

Mirror, Mirror

AD 1727 – Deutz, the Duchy of Burg Nesselrath, North Rhine-Westphalia, Prussia.

Ursula clutched at her head and the fist that gripped her hair.

She wanted to cry out, but the pain and shock limited her to a gasping whimper as she desperately staggered to stay on her feet whilst her assailant dragged her along the cold, stone corridor.

They came to a standstill at a doorway, the distinct fumbling of iron keys preceding the clank of a disengaging door latch and the grinding of neglected hinges. A painful, sharp tug seared through Ursula's scalp as she was propelled through the doorway, where she crashed painfully into the slate-tiled floor, sending a cloud of choking dust into the air. The door slammed behind her, and the lock clunked finally and solidly.

"Let this be a lesson to you," screeched Lady Millicent von Reichenstein, her voice muffled by the heavy, oak planks. "It is about time you learned some respect, young lady. I might not be your mother, but I will not be belittled by a child, do you hear me?"

"Go away," cried Ursula, tears streaming down her burning cheeks. There was no response. Lady Millicent was already gone.

Oh, how Ursula *hated* her stepmother. Lady Millicent had married her father, Lord Franz Wilhelm von Reichenstein, three years earlier and, no matter how she behaved, he believed the vile woman could do no wrong. Ursula and her father had always been close, ever since her mother had passed when she was just a young child. However, she was in no doubt that their relationship had chilled somewhat since Millicent came into their lives. And now, at sixteen, her stepmother was attempting to force Ursula from the family home entirely. That was the basis of today's quarrel. Once again, Lady Millicent had broached the subject of "introducing" Ursula to eligible gentlemen. Ursula had no interest in the parade of chinless, befuddled dimwits that seemed to constitute the upper-class bachelors of this region. She had no time for fools and could think of nothing worse than being married-off to a man she loathed. Truth be told, she had little patience for men of any description. Aside from her father, that is. She loved him with all her heart, even though he was increasingly distant of late.

Mirror, Mirror

Weak light bled through the high, narrow, leaded-glass windows, made sepia by the patina of grime that coated their surface. Ursula sat up and dusted down the bodice of her torn dress, wincing as she flexed her right arm. Her elbow was grazed, with dirt sticking to the fresh blood, whilst her knee throbbed where it had connected with the stone floor. She glanced about the rotunda, taking in her cluttered surroundings, encircled as she was by old chairs, dressers, and tables, each shrouded in white sheets, like the ghosts of furniture past. The air was filled with dust. Ursula knew this place, though she had not been here in eight long years. Not since her mother died. This was the south tower, where they had taken the former Lady von Reichenstein when she fell ill. The apothecary cared for her in the tower's highest room for two long weeks whilst the fever burned through her until it eventually took her life. Her father had allowed Ursula to see her mother just once, the day before she passed, just to say goodbye. Ursula had hardly recognised the emaciated woman in the bed, and Lady von Reichenstein did not seem to know her daughter or husband at all, so delirious was she with fever and from the drugs administered to lessen her pain. Ursula tried not to remember her mother like that, preferring to think of her at her most vital, though the memories of her mother had faded somewhat over the years. A smile, her eyes, her laugh… those were the things that remained, though Ursula did not know if those echoes were even real.

She hauled herself upright using the creaking armchair beside her and stripped it of its sheet, sending a cloud of dust into the air, wafting her hand before her face to keep the choking haze from her nose and mouth. Ursula slumped into the rickety seat and sighed. If she was going to be here for a while, she should at least get comfortable.

She woke with a start. It was dark outside now and cold as the depths of winter in here with no fireplace and no lamps to offer even a semblance of warmth. Her breath hung in the frigid air and Ursula shivered uncontrollably as she gathered up the discarded dustsheet from the ground and wrapped it around her trembling shoulders.

Something had woken her. Something in the tower's darkness. It niggled at her, picking at her soul like a scratch on the roof of her mouth. Perhaps it was no more than a dream?

She heard it again. A whisper, just on the cusp of hearing. Calling her name. Beckoning her to it. This was no dream.

Mirror, Mirror

Staving off the cramp in her legs, Ursula struggled to her feet and shuffled towards the back of the circular room. She tried the door to the tower's stairs, but it was locked, which came as no surprise; the south tower had been ruled off-limits by her father after her mother's passing and nobody came here any longer, on pain of death. All the items stored here had been her mother's: her dressing table, her wardrobe, even an old sundial that had been Lady von Reichenstein's favourite from her private ornamental garden. It had all clearly been dumped here by bloody Millicent, so desperate was she to remove every last memory of Ursula's mother.

The whisper called out again, louder this time. It emanated from the object deep at the back of the room, obscured from view by the myriad of other discarded detritus from her mother's life. The object was large, perhaps as tall, and broad as a man from the front, yet narrow when viewed from the side. Ornamental wooden feet, mounted on brass wheels, poked out from beneath the sheet. Ursula knew the object at once.

The mirror.

She remembered the day it had arrived, shortly before her mother fell ill. It was delivered by four serious-looking

Mirror, Mirror

men, wearing chain mail, swords, and grim expressions. They certainly did not have the appearance of any carpenters or tradesmen Ursula had ever seen before. Her mother had thanked the men for bringing the object to her and paid them handsomely with a large purse of golden coins, but she had shooed Ursula away when she noticed the young girl watching.

Her mother never used the mirror, and the young girl had watched from the courtyard as a pair of servants, acting on her mother's instruction, carried it, covered in this same sheet, and deposited it in the south tower. Ursula presumed it a gift for her father's upcoming birthday and thought no more of it. Not too long after, their lives fell to pieces as Lady von Reichenstein fell deathly ill, and Ursula was never given cause to think of the mirror again.

Until now.

Reaching out with tentative fingers, she gripped the sheet and tugged. Inch-by-inch the dustsheet fell away, finally falling to the ground, revealing the reflective surface beneath. Ursula gasped. For there in the mirror's silver surface, staring back at her was a woman. Was it her mother? No. It looked just like her, though not quite. This woman had thick black curls, just like Ursula herself, whereas her mother had had fine,

Mirror, Mirror

auburn hair – kissed by fire as her father often said. The mirror woman's eyes were hazel, unlike the crystal blue of her mother's. And this woman was older than her mother had been when she passed, though still beautiful. The reflection depicted the room just as it currently was, whilst the mirror woman's movements matched those of Ursula herself. Was she seeing things? Was she dreaming? And then realisation hit: The woman in the mirror was her! An older her, certainly, dressed in finery and wearing exquisite jewellery, but there was no doubt that this woman was her.

"What kind of sorcery is this?" she gasped. But, to Ursula's horror, her reflection remained unchanged, lips unmoving, except to break into an almost imperceptible smile.

"Not sorcery, Ursula," the mirror woman said, her voice seemingly coming from afar. "Enchantment."

"Who are you?" Ursula took a step back, the hair standing up on her neck, sending crackling charges running through her scalp and down her spine. The mirror woman did not, however, retreat.

"You know who I am, Ursula," the woman said.

She shook her head, her mouth dry and hands shaking with fear now, rather than from the bitter cold. "No…"

"You know what I say is true."

"It can't be..."

"And yet I am here. I am *you*, Ursula. I am older, wiser, stronger, but I am *you*. I have seen this all before. I remember being locked in here by that wicked *bitch*. I remember meeting *me*."

"Why are you here?"

"I am here to help you, Ursula," the woman said, smiling kindly, her eyes filled with benevolent warmth. "I am here to *free* you. To *guide* you."

"What do you mean?"

"You are destined for great things, Ursula," the mirror woman told her. "You will achieve things most men only dream of. You are capable of such magnificence. And with my help, you will achieve all your desires, without being beholden to any man. Otherwise, what awaits you is a life of servitude... misery... submission. Seize your destiny, Ursula!"

Ursula smiled, allowing her mind to wander for a moment. She was smarter and more capable than most. She loved her father, though believed he was drifting through his duties, making decisions based on nothing more than privileged entitlement, without considering the impacts upon those who lived within his manor. Truth be told, as long as he received his taxes, Ursula believed her father cared little for the people he was charged to serve. She would be a more capable leader than Lord von Reichenstein. Than any man for that matter.

"How?" she asked.

"That depends upon you, Ursula. On how far you are prepared to go – what steps you are prepared to take. Your potential is limitless, and only *you* can determine that."

Ursula straightened, pushed back her shoulders, and raised her chin, comporting herself just as her mother had taught her all those years before.

"I will do anything."

"Anything?"

"*Anything*," she said, jaw clenched, radiating fierce determination. "Just tell me what I must do."

The mirror Ursula nodded, gravely, as though considering her younger self's words.

"Very well," she said, finally, with seeming reluctance. "But why *tell* you when I can *show* you? Step closer."

"Show me?"

"Yes," said the mirror her. "The enchantment allows me to provide you with that knowledge. Such knowledge you can hardly comprehend. Just come to me and I will show you everything."

Taking a deep breath, Ursula stepped forward. The mirror her held out a hand, placing her fingertips against the glass. Ursula reached out, slowly, every fibre of her being telling her to stop. To turn and run away. However, she could not bear the thought of simply surrendering to this life of misery, under the yolk of her cruel stepmother.

Gripped by determination, Ursula reached out and touched the glass.

The breath caught in Ursula's throat. Panic gripped her heart as her mind was filled with terrible visions: blood, flames, gore, the sounds of swords clashing, women and children screaming, hooves on packed snow…

…until the darkness overwhelmed her.

***

Mirror, Mirror

The blaze tore through the castle's west wing like hot water through ice, releasing a heat so intense that it stung Ursula's face even from the courtyard's far side. Flames licked from every window and door and from the hole in the roof where the structure had collapsed. Ursula was completely calm, whilst those huddled around her sobbed and clung to each other as the flames licked at the night sky and plumes of thick smoke billowed into the darkness, obscuring the stars. Some of the town's men had formed bucket chains to the river, but their efforts were futile. The inferno raged on, unabated.

"I'm so sorry, Your Grace," wept Heinz, one of her father's most trusted servants. Tears streaked his soot-smeared face. "I could not reach them. The fire took hold so fast. I… I… couldn't…"

"It's okay, Heinz," she assured him, taking his hands in hers and offering him a wan smile. "I know you did everything you could. All we can do now is pray for them."

***

As with all such tragedies, after a period of mourning, life went on. Seventeen lives were lost to the flames: fifteen servants and Lord and Lady von Reichenstein. Twenty-three if you counted the poor dogs. Those that were left behind were bereft. All lost friends and family members, whilst the castle's main living quarters and kitchens were utterly razed.

All agreed that the new Lady von Reichenstein was the rock they all clung to as Ursula led them with compassion and certainty. Her strength gave them strength: through the funerals, the restoration of the castle, the rebuilding of the manor.

By eighteen, Ursula was seen as a powerhouse of local political discourse, negotiating land and trade agreements with neighbouring lords, expanding her territories, growing her influence, leading her manor into unprecedented prosperity. However, the volatile nature of the Prussian state brought with it war and opportunism, whilst some surrounding lords and barons saw a teenage girl as an easy target. And so, Ursula used the newfound wealth of her manor to strengthen her own standing forces, employing mercenaries in their hundreds to train the young men to join her army. She forged alliances with neighbouring manors, forming a formidable military horde. And every man Jack of them would die for her.

And fuelled by that passion, Ursula's army repelled everything thrown at their tiny province; from Ansbach, from Brandenburg, from Danzig, from the Poles, Hungarians, and even the mighty French.

By twenty-three, Ursula's fearsome reputation was known across the continent. Even the bravest, most successful generals avoided engaging her in battle and their political delegates knew better than to take on her wits. The world consciously left Lady von Reichenstein and her little patch of Prussia well alone.

At twenty-four, Ursula gave birth to two daughters, Claudia, and Elisabeth, though none knew the father's identity. Many rumoured they were the progeny of a dalliance with one of her mercenary commanders, whilst some peasant folk believed the twins to be of immaculate conception. Even the most ardent realist would not rule out either option. The Lady von Reichenstein was capable of anything.

At thirty-five, Ursula finally took a husband, though her marriage to the recently widowed baron was largely based on ambition rather than love. She became quite fond of Baron Philipp von und zu Erthal, principal advisor to the Prince Elector of Mainz, and he was besotted with her, so desperate was he to mend the hole in his aching heart. And the years had been kind to Ursula – her beauty was untarnished by time, her skin still soft, full, and unblemished, her dark curls lustrous, without any sign of silver threads. Her hazel eyes still shone with mischief and warmth. And to her great surprise, Ursula was happy.

However, the new Baroness von und zu Erthal was not so enamoured of her eighteen-year-old stepdaughter, Maria Sophia. The two clashed frequently, particularly regarding Claudia and Elisabeth. The girls *hated* each other. Ursula asked her daughters to at least *try* and get along with Maria Sophia, at least for the sake of her marriage to Philipp. Ursula had invested too much time and effort into obtaining the title of Baroness von und zu Erthal to allow that to be jeopardised by squabbling children. Her daughters acceded to their mother's request, though their efforts were lukewarm at best.

As for Maria Sophia, the wilful girl challenged Ursula at every turn. The baroness had the heart and ear of one of the Prussian state's most influential men at a critical, pivotal time in their nation's history. Her influence had expanded across the country, whilst her machinations to develop their political foothold still further promised to increase her husband's profile exponentially. And yet, that girl of his could still prick the man's conscience. Maria Sophia threatened to undo all of Ursula's good work to take this useless lump of a man and mould him into a preeminent leader – a driving force in their country's expansion. She must do something about that troublesome child.

After one such quarrel, Ursula dismissed her private aides and took herself away to her private chamber, clenching and unclenching her fists as she stomped the castle's cold corridors. She unlocked her chamber's heavy oaken door and slammed it behind her, where it met the frame with a satisfying, dull clap. Once alone, Ursula let out her emotions, releasing a screech of pent-up frustration. God, how Maria Sophia irritated her! In her most reflective moments, Ursula even felt some pity for the long-deceased Lady Millicent. But only a trifle. Ursula had still thoroughly enjoyed the look of shock and horror on the woman's face as she drove the dagger through her stepmother's heart, before cutting the hapless Lord von Reichenstein's fat throat. She had delighted in setting the fire that engulfed her father's chambers and, with surprising speed, her old home's west wing. It was a shame the number of servants who were caught in the blaze, of course. Good staff were hard to come by.

Mirror, Mirror

If the events of Ursula's past taught her anything, it was that she must keep a close eye on Maria Sophia. If push came to shove, Baroness von und zu Erthal must take steps to deal with the girl before she became a real hindrance to her ambitions.

"What to do, what to do?" the Baroness mused. She sauntered to the tall object covered with a black, silken sheet in her chamber's darkest recess. It was as high and broad as a man, yet quite narrow when viewed from the side. She gripped the sheet and pulled it. It slid away smoothly and dropped to the floor.

"Tell me, mirror," she said. "What should I do with such a troublesome stepdaughter? Surely you have some insight?"

The image in the mirror's surface looked up from where she sat sobbing on the floor. Her dress torn and dusty, her youthful cheeks glistened with tears, whilst her hazel eyes were puffy, swollen, and rimmed red.

"Please," pleaded young Ursula. "Please let me go. I didn't want this. This is not fair!"

A wicked smile twisted across Baroness von und zu Erthal's ruby lips and, just for a moment, her eyes became dark and foreboding – almost completely black, like two holes in the fabric of reality.

"But mirror," she gasped, her tone filled with mock outrage, "am I not the fairest of them all?"

The Beast Must Die

September, AD 1802 – Gutach Valley, der Schwarzwald (The Black Forest), Baden.

This isn't my first visit to Hornberg. Far from it. I make my living in the Schwarzwald and my skills are highly sought, so I travel through the Gutach Valley regularly and often stay at this charming village's only inn. Surrounded by verdant hills on each side, it is certainly one of the more pleasant locations in this region and a source of much of my work. However, this is the first time I've been invited here by several village municipalities at once. Something is afoot. I can smell it... sense it. It hangs in the air like my breath in the chilly, early autumn evening. Fear. Anxiety.

The usually friendly folk won't meet my gaze as I guide my horse, Walter, through the village, heading towards its only tavern – Die Verfluchten Wölfe. I hop down from Walter's saddle and hand the reins to Gustav Dannecker, the proprietors' son, and stableboy. Like the other villagers I've encountered so far, he won't look me in the eye, and he seems

The Beast Must Die

edgy, not his usual affable, chatty self at all. He usually talks my ear off about every subject under the sun. But not today.

I put that out of my mind. I have business to address, and it will not do to keep my hosts waiting.

The tavern is unusually quiet for a Thursday evening, and I welcome the roaring fire that blazes in the hearth. I order myself a beer, then wait by the fireplace, holding out my frigid palms, absorbing the fire's heat, rubbing life back into them.

"Herr Schuster?"

I turn to face the newcomer and find a short, nervous man, probably middle-aged, though his hair is still thick and dark, with no signs of greying. His slim shoulders and portly midriff speak of privilege, as do his expensive clothes.

"Please, call me Felix," I tell him, taking his proffered hand and shaking it, warmly.

"Thank you for coming, Herr... I mean... Felix. I am Freiherr Erwin Kuhl. Please, join us in the private room and I'll have Lina bring you some food. You must be starved?"

The upstairs private room is a more lavish affair than the public bar I'm more used to, with its walnut-panelled walls, dotted with paintings – hunting scenes, mostly – and the occasional portrait of the area's noblemen. Between the pair of windows stands an elegant longcase clock. Above the smaller fireplace, a stag's head dominates the room, its antler's spanning several feet across. A huge, highly polished table occupies the room's heart, with several more privileged men in attendance. Aside from the pleasant, warm aroma of woodsmoke, the room is fragranced with beeswax and a myriad of sweeter perfumes emanating from its occupants. These are not the sort of men I'm used to doing business with.

"Please, take a seat, Herr Schuster," invites Freiherr Kuhl, helpfully pulling out a high-backed chair at the table's head and gesturing for me to sit.

I glance around the room's four other occupants, each of them watching me intently. But it's the man at the table's other end who catches my attention. He's older than the others, as his white hair attests – though there isn't an ounce of frailty in him. Although of the same corpulent figure as the others, his arms are thick, and hands gnarled. Something about the way he carries himself begs me to be wary. This is not a man afraid to get his hands dirty, unlike the rest of these noble gentlemen who have probably never done a day's hard graft in their lives. However, it's his eyes that fascinate me: dark, intense, piercing... I've seen eyes on men like this before. Cold, dispassionate men. I've served under men like this all my life – dyed-in-the-wool bastards all. Men who would not think twice about killing you.

"Allow me to introduce my companions," says Kuhl, taking his place at the table. "This is Herr Karl Markgraf Friedrich," he indicates the bastard opposite. I know him by reputation – not only is he the most important man in this room but perhaps the most important man in Baden. I thought him to be older than he appears – in his seventies at least – though he could easily pass for early fifties. I once heard him described as an "enlightened despot" by an old army comrade who hailed from the Rhineland. Friedrich nods, curtly, in acknowledgement, his eyes assessing everything about me. Judging me. From my shabby clothes, and long, greasy hair, to my three-day stubble, and well-worn riding boots. I can't help but feel like a child: worthless, stupid, eager to impress. I quickly gather myself and choke down that feeling.

"We also have Herr Ludwig Graf Voigt of neighbouring Steinenbach, Herr Otto Graf Krämer of Neiderwasser, and, of course, Father Maier of our local parish."

"We're already acquainted," scowls the priest. His holiness and I have had several run-ins over the years.

"Thank you for inviting me, gentlemen," I say, using my most gracious tone. "It's not often I meet with such exalted company on my travels. Can I ask why you wished to see me?"

"It is rather a delicate matter, Herr Schuster—" started Kuhl, though he was cut off by Friedrich.

"You're a hunter, are you not?"

"I make my living in many ways, Herr Markgraf Friedrich. Hunting is just one of them."

Each passage of Friedrich's speech is punctuated by a pause whilst he visually assesses me. A technique I am familiar with – designed to disconcert. To trip me up in an urge to fill the uncomfortable silence. I won't fall into that trap. I hold my tongue. And my nerve.

"Dangerous beasts and whatnot?"

"Beasts, pests, men," I shrug. "I go where the money is."

Friedrich nods, seemingly satisfied with my response. I squirm in my seat, waiting for him to speak again. No one has put me on edge like this in my adult life. Something about his eyes fills me with unease, though judging by the deferential expressions of his companions, they feel the same way. Friedrich catches Kuhl's eye and gestures to proceed with a

The Beast Must Die

lugubrious wave of a hand. Outside, the sonorous chime of church bells reverberate around the valley. I look at the clock in puzzlement – it's only a quarter past six.

"Sunset," says Father Maier, reading my intrigued expression. "Curfew."

"Curfew?"

"Yes," confirms Kuhl. "We have experienced some… unfortunate incidents in recent months. We have taken the precaution of confining the populace in Hornberg and surrounding villages to their homes after dark."

"Pah!" spat Krämer. "For what good it has done."

"Gentlemen, please," I interrupt. "I am still unsure why you seek my services. Or even *if* you seek my services."

Voigt clears his throat and picks up the conversation. "Apologies, Herr Schuster, we do indeed wish to employ your expertise. What my honourable friend here has failed to articulate is the nature of these *incidents*. Murders!"

"Murders?" I ask, intrigued. This job may be interesting after all.

"Can a beast commit murder?" asks Maier.

"Beast?" I say. "I'm sorry, gentlemen, you are losing me again."

"It started in June," sighed Kuhl. "Three bodies, each savagely mutilated over three nights. Discovered in the streets. Torn apart. One in each of our villages."

"Interesting," I muse. "Could these not be isolated incidents?"

"That's what we believed," says Krämer. "Until almost one month later, when the same thing occurred."

"Three more bodies," picks up Kuhl. "Two here in Hornberg and one in Neiderwasser. Six murders, a month apart, all coinciding with the full moon."

"Though we have heard rumours of similar incidents in other towns and villages along the Rhine. Always close to the forest and all on the same three days," adds Voigt.

"And so," says Kuhl, "with the assistance of Herr Markgraf Friedrich, we instituted the curfew throughout Baden."

The room falls into silence again, as each of the civic leaders exchange more nervous glances.

"There's more?" I ask. They are holding back on the details, I know. But why? They almost seem… embarrassed?

"The attacks continued," says Kuhl. "We expected some people to break curfew, of course, but…" his voice falters again.

"But what?" I snap, unable to keep the impatience from my tone.

"Four murders last month, at the full moon," says Kuhl. "Each of them children. One in Hornberg, two in Steinenbach – twins – and another in Neiderwasser. Taken from their beds, mutilated, murdered, then discarded in the forest."

There was that word again. Murder. Not usually a verb one would associate with an animal.

"Taken from their beds, you say?" I ask. "That does not sound like any beast I know."

"What do you know of wolves, Herr Shuster?" chimes in Friedrich.

"Wolves?" I snort. "Only that there aren't many of them left in the Schwarzwald. We've hunted bears and wolves almost to extinction. Those wolves that remain tend to stay well away from humans and our settlements. There is no shortage of food in the forest."

"The wolves we speak of are different," says Kuhl. "They are savage and terrible – more human than animal."

"Werwolf!" hisses Krämer.

"Werwolf?" I scoff, unable to restrain my amusement. "Gentlemen, I have travelled throughout this region for many years, and I have heard every folk tale a hundred times over. That is all they are: stories told by the ignorant and believed by the credulous. In my experience, the most terrible atrocities are committed by ordinary men."

"No ordinary man is capable of such carnage," mutters Voigt, his voice thick, and his fist held genteelly before his mouth, as though holding back the urge to vomit.

"You would be very surprised, sir," I tell him. "I have seen my fellows commit the very worst of outrages. War brings this out in a man. Once released, sometimes the beast within the man cannot be tamed."

"I assure you, Herr Schuster," says Kuhl, "no man is responsible for these crimes. And it is no coincidence that each of these killings was perpetrated at the full moon. Please, Herr Schuster, allow me to show you."

They lead me out of the room and along the inn's familiar corridor. I have stayed here many times and have probably slept in most of these rooms. But not this one. These last few rooms, their doors painted a distinct blue, are reserved for the Dannecker family and their staff, whilst the landlord and lady occupy the attic apartment. We reach the door at the corridor's end and Kuhl extracts a key from his waistcoat pocket and unlocks it. It swings open with an ominous creak. The room beyond is not like the inn's other modest accommodations. Dolls and toys are neatly arranged in mid-play, whilst a large replica of the tavern sits beneath one of the two small windows. I tentatively step into the room and approach the model house. I flick open the latch and the building's facia swings open on smooth hinges. Inside are several intricately modelled rooms, including furniture and carved wooden figures, dressed in charming, handmade clothing. It really is an example of fine craftsmanship.

"I made this for Gretchen's last birthday," comes a hoarse voice from the doorway. I turn to find Ulrich Dannecker, the landlord. He looks much older than I last remember him: his features have a haunted expression, and his puffy eyes are red-rimmed and glistening. He lights a taper and busies himself igniting the oil lamp on the dresser. "Gus helped carve the dolls and Lina made the clothes, the curtains, and the bedsheets. Gretchen loved it so."

Realisation hits like icy water, and I understand why they have brought me here. Why the townspeople are so withdrawn. Why the Dannecker family seem so lost. They are in mourning.

"Uli," I say. "I'm so sorry..."

The landlord just nods, dolefully. A single tear runs down his cheek and mingles with the bristles of his unshaven muzzle.

"My girl was just seven. She never hurt anyone..." he starts, his bottom lip trembling uncontrollably. Then he looks me in the eye. "Just find the monster who did this, Felix. Please excuse me, gentlemen."

With that, Uli hurries from the room. No wonder the people here are so shaken up. Hornberg is a small village – one of those places where everyone knows everyone else – and a tragedy like this would affect them all, intimately.

"Over here," says Kuhl, leading me to the other window. He snaps open the latch and pushes it wide open, before illuminating the sill with his lamp. I peer closely, but I can see right away what the freiherr wants to show me: gouged into the hardwood, two sets of four deep scratches, as though caused by clawed fingers.

"Claw marks?" Kuhl nods and leads me over to the bed.

"And here," he says, shining the torch on the bedpost. And sure enough, another set of uneven grooves, scored into the timber frame.

"There was blood too," he says, wiping a tear from his eye. "And what they did to her... No godly creature is capable of such a thing."

"Can I see the body?" I ask. I'm keen to know what I'm dealing with, and bite marks might tell me a story of the creature's size.

"No," says Friedrich. "The bodies have been burned. Just to be sure."

"Sure of what?"

"Perhaps we should return to the private room?" urges Kuhl. "This has been a painful time for the Dannecker family.

It would not be prudent to discuss such things where they may hear."

"Okay," I say, back in the private room. "You want me to hunt down your beast? How much will you pay me?"

The men exchange looks once more, though this time, they're all looking to one man: Friedrich.

"One hundred gulden each day for your time and inconvenience. Thirty thousand when you bring me the beast's head," he says, with the smirk of a man to whom that is small change, but knows, for me, that is more than I can earn in several years. I try to contain my surprise, though the message does not make it to my eyebrows, which threaten to merge with my hairline.

"You really want this beast," I say.

"We do," admits Kuhl. "And Herr Markgraf Friedrich has been kind enough to put up the reward for your services. I will also, of course, cover your stay here, including your food. For all of you gentlemen too."

"Very gracious of you, Herr Kuhl," I say over the chorus of mumbled appreciation. "So, we're all staying here?"

"Well, all except me," says Kuhl. "I live nearby. I will return home to my wife and children."

"Is that wise?" asks Krämer. "After all, curfew has been called."

"It is but a short walk," Kuhl assures him. "Though I must stress, Herr Schuster, time is of the essence. You must begin your work tonight. Today sees the first full moon, meaning you have just three days to track this beast down and kill it or we must wait another month for an opportunity. How many more will die?"

I drain my stein and plonk it back on the table's polished surface. My stomach rumbles – I still haven't eaten.

"Gentlemen, if you will excuse me? I wish to rest and prepare myself for the evening's hunt. If someone can show me to my room and arrange for some food, please?"

"Of course, please forgive me, Herr Schuster," says Kuhl. "I will arrange it immediately."

"I will show Herr Schuster to his room," offers Friedrich, and the hackles rise on my neck and arms. The thought of being alone in a room with this man troubles something deep inside my primal hindbrain. What is it about him? I smile as warmly as I can manage and allow the man to escort me into the corridor and a few doors along to a small, pleasant room. It has already been prepared and my bags and weapons have been brought up and placed at the bed's foot. A lamp burns on the dresser, casting its pale, yellow glow, making the shadows dance in the corners.

"Schnapps?" the markgraf asks, pouring himself a generous measure.

"No, thank you, Herr Markgraf."

"Please, call me Karl," he says, sipping the spirit. "And what should I call you, Herr Schuster?"

"Felix."

"Felix…" he muses. "You're a military man, Herr Schuster." It's a statement rather than a question, yet I feel compelled to answer.

"Yes, sir."

"As am I, Felix. You fought against the French?"

"Yes, sir."

"I assume you have seen many terrible, terrible things in that time? You have witnessed exactly what horrors a man is capable of?"

"I have, sir," I say. And I can tell by his smirk that he knows I have committed as many atrocities in my time at war as I have observed. He can *read* me. It is as though his cool, obdurate gaze can penetrate my very soul.

"These are turbulent times, Felix," he says, pouring himself another measure. "Baden has seen much tribulation these past decades. But we are a progressive people. We are stronger together – in unity, we almost prevailed against the mighty French army. We pushed them back and held the lands east of the Rhine. Next year I will be appointed elector of this region, and we will forge stronger links with the Rhineland and other states. We cannot allow any small inconvenience to derail that, Felix. Even a single grain of sand can stop the finest watch."

"I understand, sir."

"Find this monster, Felix," he says, his expression turning hard, focused. "Find it and kill it. We must have a culprit so our children may rest easy in their beds once more."

A knock at the door breaks the tension, and I'm grateful for the disruption. I open it, and Lina, the landlady, brings in a plate of cooked meats, bread, and sauerkraut and sets it on the nightstand. Friedrich bids me good night and leaves me alone with my food and my thoughts.

The moon is high in the sky, casting its cool light over the landscape as Walter and I reach the forest's periphery. He's unusually jittery and nervous and doesn't want to go any further, so I dismount and tie him to a thick pine at the apron. I stroke his muzzle and whisper calming words to soothe him, then fasten his nosebag in place. He's a good horse – my faithful companion and only friend for over five years now. I feel his trepidation, but I have thirty-thousand good reasons for braving the forest at night, even though every fibre of my being screams at me to ride for the hills. I know better than to go back on my word when such powerful men are concerned. If I betray them, my livelihood is as good as over.

A light frost has settled over everything, and I'm chilled to the bone despite my thick layers of leather and fleece. My boots crunch on the needles which have formed a carpet over the forest floor. Keen eyes adjusting to the darkness, looking for any movement, I unshoulder my crossbow, place my foot in the stirrup and draw back the string until it locks in place.

Then I slide a fresh bolt into the groove, ready to fire upon any beast with murderous intent.

Only Markgraf Friedrich didn't seem to have an issue with my plan to venture into the Schwarzwald in search of the creature. I reasoned that this werwolf – if there is such a thing – had struck in three different villages that we know of, meaning I had no idea where to begin. Therefore, my best and only option was to start at its home. Every forest creature leaves behind traces: footprints, faeces, the remains of its prey. For some reason, the image of those claw marks comes back into my mind, and I have to shake my head to dislodge them.

After an hour, the temperature has dropped further still, and my flask of glühwein has long since lost its heat. Still, I savour the last few drops of the sour liquid from the flimsy bladder, then tuck it back into my pack. The forest is quiet – unnervingly so. Even at night, there's usually more movement as nocturnal beasts go about their nightly business. It's as though even the landscape is holding its breath – afraid to draw unwanted attention.

Just then, something flashes across my peripheral vision, off to my left, and I raise my crossbow and fire. I chide myself for my nervous, amateurish reaction, shooting before locking sight on my target. It is not like me. The tension seems to be affecting even a seasoned campaigner such as I. Muttering, I follow my bolt's path to the tall pine where it has buried itself in an unfortunate squirrel, pinning it to the trunk. Still, I can take pride in a good, instinctive shot, especially in the dark – right through the rodent's neck. I wrench the bolt from the tree and put the dead squirrel in my pack. I might be glad of the meat one day soon.

As I prepare to re-draw my bow, I get that feeling – the one that has helped me survive two decades of killing them before they kill me. Someone is watching me. Someone, or some*thing*.

Slowly, surreptitiously, I scan the treeline, looking for anything out of place. I turn my head, and then I see it, just for a moment – the glint of eyes, reflecting the moonlight. By the time I've reloaded my bow, they're gone. But I know it wasn't my imagination. I heard the scuffle of feet on the pine needles and, as I hurry in my observer's direction, the branches of a nearby bush still sway from their recent disturbance. It was here. Watching me. For how long, I do not know.

I follow the trail of disturbed needles and broken branches for several more yards until I lose any sense of which direction it may have gone.

One thing is for sure, it knows I was here. And I would hazard it knows why.

Dawn's lascivious tendrils spread their loving embrace across the land as Walter and I return to Hornberg, ready for my warm bed. I saw no more signs of my mysterious watcher and neither did I sense its presence. My best guess is that I scared it back to wherever the beast holes up during the day. However, I used my time to leave it some surprises should it come sneaking out again.

The sleepy village is already wide awake when I arrive – there's a commotion outside the tavern and I can see Krämer and Voigt trying to calm down the crowd. A chill runs down my spine and I know the beast has struck again.

"Come with me," growls Krämer, without salutation and he storms across the street, following the narrow lane between the houses opposite. I hand Walter's reins to Gus with a heartfelt thanks and follow after Krämer and Voigt, my heart pounding so hard I can almost hear it.

"While you were swanning around the forest at night, playing Wod the Huntsman, the beast was here, wreaking havoc again," Krämer snarled.

"What's happened?" I ask, though both men ignore me and continue their earnest march. We turn right at the next intersection, where stands Friedrich, standing over…

"Oh…"

"Oh, indeed," scowls Voigt. "His poor wife."

Sprawled across the cobbled pavement that runs between two cottages, lies the body of Freiherr Erwin Kuhl. His eyes are still wide open, his expression set in a rictus of terror. His body is torn open from sternum to pelvis, innards spilling out in a mass of scarlet gore. One leg is bent at an odd angle, whilst both wrists are snapped at ninety degrees. The spatter of blood around the place where his throat should be, indicates the likely cause of death. The disembowelling seemingly followed afterwards.

"You should have been here, Schuster," snaps Krämer. "This is your fault!"

"That's enough," interjects Friedrich, levelly. "This is no more Herr Schuster's fault than it is yours or mine."

"When did this happen?" I ask, my head spinning, exhaustion weighing heavy on my soul.

"He left us shortly before ten last evening," confirms Friedrich. "His wife says he never made it home."

I pinch the bridge of my nose and groan inwardly. Kuhl was likely dead even before I set off for the forest.

"Surely someone heard the attack?" I say.

"Apparently, no one heard a thing," shrugs Friedrich.

"Okay," I sigh. "I want you to set up nightly patrols – use trusted men, those who know how to handle a weapon. Patrols must always be in pairs, never alone. Have them on three-hour rotations through the night in all three villages."

"Isn't that what we're paying you for?" scowls Voigt.

"No, you're paying me for my expertise, Herr Graf Voigt," I retort. "Appoint one man to take charge and organise each patrol. I want them to report back to me each morning. If they see anything, I want to know about it."

"You heard the man," says Friedrich, and Krämer and Voigt scurry off to attend to their instructions. It feels good to order those pompous pea-counters around.

"Thank you, sir."

"Don't mention it," says Friedrich. "Please do not think too harshly of them. They mean well, but they have lost a close friend. They want this beast found, Felix."

"We all do, sir."

"Quite. What news of your hunt? Anything?"

"I saw something, sir," I tell him of my encounter with my mysterious observer. Friedrich purses his lips, nodding thoughtfully.

"You have the beast scared," he says, eventually. "But it's wily… cunning… dangerous. Perhaps as crafty a hunter as you yourself, Felix. What next?"

"I have some surprises in store for our friend," I tell him. "We start the patrols tonight and I will track it through the forest again. I found several trails last night, though they didn't go far. The beast covers its tracks – even sets false trails for hunters like me to follow. Quite unlike anything I've ever encountered, sir."

"You can catch it, can't you, Felix?" he asks me. "As I told you, we must have a culprit."

"I have never failed to obtain my quarry, sir."

"Very good, Felix," he says, smiling warmly, seemingly satisfied with my show of false confidence. "Now, get some sleep. I need you fresh for the hunt this evening. I am away on business later today, though I will return tomorrow. You can update me on progress then."

"Of course, Herr Markgraf Friedrich."

"Thank you, Felix." Friedrich sighs and shakes his head, staring in sombre fashion at what's left of the recently departed Freiherr of Hornberg. "I had better make arrangements for Herr Kuhl's remains. His poor wife and children."

As I make my way back to the tavern, something niggles at my exhausted brain. Something I should have noticed. It's there, lurking in the recesses of my mind, peering out at me, piquing my interest, but whenever I try to think about it, it ducks out of sight again.

I'm just sliding into sleep's warm embrace when it grabs me by the shoulders and shakes me awake. I sit up, eyes wide, fatigue washed away in an instant as I realise what my brain was attempting to alert me to.

Kuhl's body – despite his terrible injuries and horrific evisceration, there was a complete absence of claw or bite marks. I walk over to the window and draw open the curtains.

From the village outskirts, the dark smoke of Kuhl's funeral pyre curls into the sky.

My first task upon arriving in the Schwarzwald on my second night was to check the traps I laid the previous evening. I set thirty foothold traps around the forest floor at strategic points between Steinenbach and Neiderwasser. They're nasty things, comprising a pair of sprung iron jaws that will snap shut on anything heavy enough to trigger the mechanism. Anything bigger than a rabbit should set it off. It would likely break the ankle and significantly inconvenience anything human-sized. And unless they're smart enough to disengage the jaws, they're not going anywhere, as each heavy trap is chained to a nearby tree. I hate using these things, as I invariably catch something other than my target quarry, though they are an incredibly effective weapon in the hunter's arsenal.

Just two of the traps have triggered – both of them near Steinenbach to the north of Hornberg: the first was triggered by a hare – which I stow in my bag for later – whilst the second I discover contains the dismembered lower leg of something a little bigger. A dog perhaps? Or could it be a wolf? Judging by the ragged injury, the desperate creature seems to have gnawed off the broken limb to escape. I follow the trail of blood several hundred yards, where I find the poor beast. It is a dog – a large one, though smaller than any wolf. Probably living wild in the forest. It's certainly not big enough to be our culprit. It's just an ordinary dog.

The rest of the evening is uneventful, as Walter and I make our way south, checking the traps and searching for any other signs of our killer. Tonight is a quiet one, and I have no more sense of my mysterious observer's presence.

At first light, I head back to Hornberg, my stomach churning at the prospect of what might be waiting upon my return. But there is no commotion today, and I'm able to go to my bed and sleep the sleep of the just. The just exhausted.

I awake that afternoon to news from Steinenbach – there was another abduction and murder that evening. A child again, taken from their ground-floor bedroom. He was just eight years old.

I take a ride north, accompanied by Herr Graf Voigt, and head to the small town to investigate. Once again, the window's sill is scored with claw marks.

"It's a terrible thing," Voigt tells me. "They're all looking to me for answers, Herr Schuster. I've told them you're close to solving this. You will find the beast, won't you?"

"I hope so, Herr Voigt," I tell him. "I've never seen anything like this."

I'm drawn back to the window, and my fingers trace the rough grooves, gouged into the wood. Why would there be claw marks here? I mean, Gretchen's room was on the second storey, so the beast would have had to climb up to her room. In that regard, the scratches made sense. However, this is a ground-floor room, and the sill is only a few feet from the ground. Why would the beast have need to scratch the sill? Such perfectly regulated grooves too – identical to those outside Gretchen's window.

Still, I put that to the back of my mind, and Voigt and I head out to the forest where the local search party found the boy's body.

"Just like the others," Voigt tells me, covering his mouth and nose with his handkerchief. "The beast has eaten the poor child's heart, liver, and kidneys."

Like Kuhl, the small boy's torso has been torn open and viscera spills out from the gaping wound like grotesque sausage links. Flies buzz around the corpse. Where his eyes should be are two gory sockets – probably plucked out by crows, judging by their piercing caws from the surrounding trees, frightened away by the group of men attending to the body.

"Removed," I correct Voigt.

"I'm sorry?"

"The organs have been removed, yes. We don't know if they've been eaten. Look at the wounds – no visible claw marks, no bite marks. Aside from the post-mortem injuries inflicted by the crows, there are no other signs of animal attack. I've seen thousands of wolf and bear attacks on people, deer, boar. This does not resemble any of them. Animals kill for food. They rarely operate with such precision – and as horrific as this is, they rarely leave the body so... clean. Wolves are pack creatures. I would expect to find little in the way of remains."

"Just find this beast, Herr Schuster," said Voigt, an edge of pleading in his voice. "We have seen too much tragedy in these parts in recent months. I do not know how much more our people can take."

As I head back to Walter, Voigt orders the men of Steinenbach to burn the boy's body. I make my way back to Hornberg alone, giving me time with my thoughts to digest these latest events. It is the last night of full moon. If I do not find the beast tonight, it will be another month until it resurfaces, and I will have to start all over again. If the villagers don't lynch me first, that is.

Within moments of my arrival in the forest, I can sense it. My observer. The night is deathly quiet again, as though the local fauna dare not draw attention – though whether they are more afraid of *it* or *me*, I do not know. I cannot see it, nor hear it, but I know it is *there*. Nearby, watching my every move.

Suddenly, I hear the unmistakable, metallic snap of a trap, accompanied by a cry of pain. I sprint towards it, careful not to set an errant foot in one of my other traps. I find the metal jaws, although there is no sign of the creature. The heavy, iron jaws are mangled, torn apart as though insubstantial as paper, though their teeth are smeared red. Whatever this beast is, it is strong. And it is injured.

Just then, I see a movement. Something slips through the shadows, a darker shape, disturbing the undergrowth, moving quickly. I heft my crossbow and head after it. It moves fast, frequently changing direction, though making enough noise now that I can track it easily. It's frightened, abandoning all attempts at stealth.

I hear another clang, up ahead, and a second cry of pain. Higher pitched than the last. Moments later I'm upon it. The beast lies on the ground, clutching its leg. Beside it, another shape takes flight, disappearing into the trees.

What lies before me is the strangest creature I have ever seen. It is human in shape, though with dog-like facial features: an elongated snout, with wide, tooth-filled jaws beneath a black, glistening nose and deep-set eyes that shine as they catch the moonlight. Pointy ears protrude through the thick, coarse fur that covers its face, head, hands and, I presume, body. It's hard to be certain as the creature is clad in a brown cotton jerkin, trousers, and black boots. It clutches at its ankle with clawed fingers, hissing and crying in pain. It is much smaller than I expected. If it were human, I'd guess it was no older than twelve.

It was true. Everything they told me. There are such things as werwolf.

"Let me go," it snarls. "Please!"

"You can speak?" I say, the pitch of my voice raised in incredulity.

"I was just thinking the same about you," it sneers. It's voice too... not at all animalistic. It sounds just like a young boy.

This one clearly did not set off the other trap.

"How many of you are there?" I ask.

"There's just me," he says. His teeth gritted. Tears roll down his fur-covered cheeks.

"I saw at least one other."

"You are mistaken," he insists. "Please! This hurts so much! Let me go!"

"I can't. You've killed people." My voice falters. I find it hard to believe this creature could have been responsible for such carnage.

"I have never killed anyone!" he screeches. "Rabbit, hare, deer – that is all. The occasional boar. My people stay away from humans."

"So, there *are* more of you?"

"No!" he starts. "Yes! Yes, of course there are. But I will never tell you where to find them. I would rather die!"

The words of Markgraf Friedrich echo in my head. "We must have a culprit," I mutter to myself, hardly realising that I spoke them aloud.

"What?" demands the werwolf. "What do you mean?"

"Never mind," I say, shaking my head.

I straddle the creature, feet set on either side of the trap, and grip its shoulder. It struggles and claws at my arm, piercing the heavy waxed fabric of my coat and penetrating the skin.

"Bloody hold still!" I hiss.

I grit my teeth, jaw set in determination. I draw my knife, raise it aloft, and stab it down with all my strength.

***

"Ah, do come in, Felix," says Friedrich from behind the ornate desk of his temporary office in the tavern's study. He stays seated and gestures to the chair opposite. "Please, help yourself to schnapps or cheese. Or I can have Lina bring you something more substantial if you prefer?" He picks up the small silver bell from the desk's surface and holds it expectantly.

"No, thank you, Herr Markgraf Friedrich," I say. "I am very tired. This will not take long."

I heft the hessian sack in my hand and drop it on the desktop before Friedrich. It makes a solid thud as it lands, then falls to one side.

"You have found our culprit?" he asks, a faint smile playing across his lips.

"Oh yes, Herr Friedrich," I say, my tone exuding certainty. "I found him."

My, What Big Teeth You Have

Late summer, early nineteenth century, Vosges, Alsace-Lorraine, Imperial Territory of the German Empire.

Casper propped his axe against the fir's trunk and mopped his brow whilst he caught his breath. The forest was eerily quiet, with only the chopping of his axe and grunts of effort, interspersed with the occasional call of a bird, chatter of a squirrel, and the gentle rustle of the breeze through the canopy above. Above all, he was grateful for the shade down here in the thick of the wood on this grotesquely warm summer day.

Men of the Arp family had been woodcutters in this region for generations, and Casper loved his work. He was sociable enough, but there was nothing like the solitude of the forest, with only the local wildlife for company. It was peaceful and restful, away from the hubbub of town.

Yet still, there was a brittle quality to the serenity. It was *too* quiet, almost as though nature was deliberately staying silent lest it attract unwanted attention.

A gaggle of geese passed overhead, just above the treetops, their tuneless honking breaking the silence and shaking Casper from his reverie.

He resumed chopping, delivering expertly timed blows to the same wedge of exposed wooden flesh until he was happy it was ready to fall. Casper braced his shoulder against it and the tree crashed to the ground with a satisfying crackle, snap, and thud.

As the fallen tree's echo faded, something else caught Casper's attention. A voice, calling out, just on the cusp of hearing. It sounded panicked, crying for help. Casper turned his head, this way and that, attempting to ascertain the direction from which the voice came. It was moving closer. Growing louder with each passing moment.

Axe hefted in both hands, he moved towards the voice and the sound of running feet, crunching across the mulch of dried needles that carpeted the forest floor. Panting breaths, as though they were terrified. It called again. No, *she* called again. It was a girl's voice. And then he saw her – a blur of red through the trees. He sprinted towards her, intercepting the path of her flight.

My, What Big Teeth You Have

Casper stepped out into one of the forest's many naturally worn paths, just ahead of the girl. She stopped, obviously startled by the sight of the large, bearded man with his shaggy mane of mousy hair and sweat-soaked, grimy clothes and clutching an axe across his chest. The girl gave a start of terror, so he carefully placed the axe on the ground before him.

"It's okay," he called, as the girl turned to run the other way. "I won't hurt you. What is wrong, little one?"

"My... my grandmother," the girl sobbed. "We were attacked. I got away but..." With that, the young girl fell to her knees, hands over her face, shoulders shaking with terrible sobs.

"It's okay," soothed Casper, advancing towards her, careful not to scare her away. The girl could have been no older than ten or eleven, clad in a bright red riding cloak and hood over an old-fashioned, washed-out yellow dress with a lace trim. Her hair, or what he could see of it beneath her hood was chestnut brown. "Where did this happen?"

"At my grandmother's cottage, not far from here," she whimpered. "I can take you. Please help us."

My, What Big Teeth You Have

Casper followed the girl until they arrived at a small cottage. There were many such dwellings like this dotted around the forest, though most were abandoned and derelict. This one was clean, tidy, and clearly lived in.

"Wait here," he whispered. He pushed at the ajar front door with the head of his axe and peered inside. Seeing no clear threats, Casper entered the cottage and looked around. There were no signs of disturbance in the single-roomed building. The wooden bed which occupied one side of the room was made, its linen's crisply and lovingly pulled taut around the straw mattress. The kitchen that comprised the cabin's other half was spotless and scrubbed clean and the fireplace had been scraped clean of soot. Someone took good care of this home.

The boards creaked as he crept across them, looking for any sign of the girl's grandmother or the beast she spoke of, but there were none.

"Hello? Little girl?" he called, realising he had not even asked her name. "Where did you see this beast? Are you sure—"

Casper's voice ran dry as he turned to face the doorway. There, blocking out the light was a tall, rangy creature, with dog-like features, pointed ears, and covered head-to-toe in

My, What Big Teeth You Have

chestnut fur. It stood on its hind legs, its muzzle bared, revealing terrible, sharp teeth. Around its neck, it wore a red riding cloak with a matching hood.

With a low growl, the beast lunged at Casper. He swung his axe, but the creature easily batted it from his hands and shoved him, until he crashed into the wall and slid down it, gasping for breath.

The beast pounced. He expected it to tear at him – to sink its dreadful teeth into his throat. Instead, it unclasped its cloak and carefully wrapped it around him, before fastening the catch around his neck. Then it gripped Casper's hair and cracked his head against the wall.

As Casper's vision faded into unconsciousness, the beast was gone. In its place stood an old woman, ancient and wrinkled, with dry, straw-like hair, and leathery skin, as naked as the day she was born. Tears welled in her eyes as she spoke.

"I'm so sorry," she croaked, as the blackness overwhelmed him.

***

Casper woke, clutching at his throbbing head. Using the wall for support, he clambered to his feet and sat on the bed's edge to gather his wits. He rubbed his eyes, then patted his face, which felt strange to the touch. Where had his beard gone? He looked at his hands, which were smaller and younger than before – those of a small child. And his garb had changed, to short-pants and matching coat, like his mother made him wear to church as a boy. Around his shoulders was draped the girl's red cloak.

"What is happening to me?" he cried, though his voice was reedy and high pitched.

And then Casper understood his fate. He had heard this story before, told by his father at bedtime, though he always believed it to be a fairy tale. But it was no child's tale – it was true. He was cursed to wander the forest, waylaying unfortunate travellers, until he could one day pass the curse to another.

Casper's stomach growled with a hunger unlike any he had ever felt.

***

The old woman staggered through the forest, clutching a sheet around her frail, naked body. She had long since ceased sobbing – she had no more tears to cry – though the guilt gnawed at her soul for condemning that poor young man to such a terrible fate. And yet, she had no choice. The weight of a century had crushed her spirit and she had to escape the curse... and the only way to do so was to pass it to another. The hunger had become all-consuming. She was losing herself. She could barely remember who she was – who she had *been* – before all of this. She had been just a young woman back then, madly in love with her new husband, forced to watch as the beast tore him apart before her eyes. For some reason, it spared her. Or so she thought. Instead, the creature forced her to wear its cloak. And when she had awoken, she was transformed into a younger version of herself – a mere girl. That was bad enough, not considering the transfiguration into something altogether more terrible when the hunger became too much. And she had taken *so* many lives these past hundred years.

Enough was enough. She was free. But at what cost?

She slumped against the rough bark of the nearest tree and slid down it, her legs no longer able to support her weight. She was so tired. So very, very tired.

"Hello, Blanchette," said a warm, soothing voice.

Blanchette looked upon her companion, attempting to focus her weary eyes, scarcely realising he had been present before he announced himself. He was tall and slim, clad in black robes. He removed his hood, revealing a bald pate and handsome face, with kindly eyes. His skin was darker than any man whom she had met before. Of course! Blanchette was her name. She had not heard it in so long.

"Who are you?" she croaked, her voice dry and raspy.

The man crouched beside her, taking her hands in his and stroking her paper-thin, mottled skin with his thumbs.

"I am here to help you, Blanchette," he said. "You have suffered for so long. You must be exhausted?"

"I am so very tired," she said, fresh tears welling in her eyes. "I just want to sleep."

"Then sleep, sweet child," he cooed, gently kissing her forehead.

She smiled, gratefully and gripped his soft hands. From here she could see the man was covered in a network of terrible scars, across his neck, ears, wrists – in fact, any visible area of skin. He must have suffered so. Blanchette felt a kindred spirit in this kind stranger. She nodded and allowed her eyes to drift shut, as the sounds and smells of the forest faded to nothingness.

The Watcher

August, AD 1802 – der Schwarzwald (The Black Forest), near Steinenbach, Baden.

"What could possibly have done such a thing?" asked Hanna, wiping fresh tears from the soft, fine fur of her cheeks.

Henrich took his wife's hand in his and squeezed it, comfortingly. "I do not know, meine geliebte. Something terrible. But I know this: no creature of the forest is capable of such a thing."

Before them, splayed out on the forest floor, lay the dismembered, corrupted bodies of two young children, perhaps six years of age. Twins perhaps? They both had the same mousy hair and pale blue eyes. They were younger than his own children. Whatever had done this had ripped the children open, exposing their innards. Henri sniffed the air – in addition to the overpowering, metallic stench of blood, he could smell the perpetrator: faintly perfumed, like sandalwood and spice. And there was something else. Not so much a scent as a feeling. Something dark. Something... *evil*. He sniffed again. There was someone else. Someone close by. Someone familiar. Two someones, in fact. He inhaled, teeth clenched and released the breath as a frustrated sigh.

"Sebastien and Monika Werner – come out and show yourselves immediately!"

After a moment, the bushes rustled and out stepped Henrich and Hanna's children, ears flattened to their heads in expectation of their father's wrath. Their mother positioned herself between her children and the mutilated bodies, to partially obstruct their view, but Henrich knew they had already seen the atrocity.

"Why are you here?" he asked, though the sullen pair simply shrugged, failing to meet their father's gaze.

"Let me put it another way," he sighed. "Where are you supposed to be?"

"At home," the pair chorused.

"That's correct. At home. And didn't I tell you not to go outside tonight under any circumstances?"

"Yes, Father," they intoned.

"Then why have you ignored my instruction?"

The Watcher

"It was all Seb's fault," blurted out Monika. At fourteen, she was two years Sebastien's senior and, though still a head taller than her brother, he was rapidly catching her up. "I told him not to follow you, but he wouldn't listen… and then—"

Henrich held up a hand, silencing his daughter's protests.

"Come here," he said.

"Henri, no!" cried Hanna. "They're just children."

"They need to see, Hanna. They must understand."

Henrich led his children forward so they could see the disembowelled bodies. Monika gasped, her hands covering her mouth. However, Seb's eyes simply widened, more in fascination than horror, Henri thought.

"Now do you see?" he asked his children. "Do you see why I told you to stay home? Do you see what humans are capable of? What do you think they would do if they found *you*?"

"What is our rule when the moon is full, children?" asked Hanna.

"When the moon full shines, we must stay inside," Monika and Sebastien recited in sing-song voices.

"That's right," their father confirmed. "Humans do not understand us, and they fear what they do not understand. They see us as feral creatures, to be slaughtered on sight. And to justify their prejudice, they invent stories of our supposed crimes. So, during the full moon, you will stay at home after dark. Especially now. There is a darkness over the Schwarzwald – I can feel it. And it grows stronger these past months. I am your father, and it is my job to keep you safe, so you will do exactly as I tell you, do you hear me?"

"Yes, father. I'm sorry," said Monika.

"Seb?"

"Fine," grumbled the younger child.

"I want your word, Sebastien," chided Hanna.

"I will stay at home," sulked the young werwolf.

"See that you do," said Henrich. "Now, Monika, take your brother home right away. Your mother and I will follow on."

"Yes, father."

His children disappeared into the forest's darkness, heading home via an indirect, weaving route, covering their tracks as they went, just as Henrich had taught them. He worried for Seb – he was a mischievous pup, fascinated with God's creation and particularly curious of the human world of which they could never be a part. He reminded Henrich of his younger brother, Stefan – and the fear that his son would meet the same grizzly end haunted him. Henrich tried not to be *too* authoritarian, like his and Stefan's father had been, fearing that Seb would rebel in the same manner as both he and his brother. All Henrich asked was that his children stayed inside at night during the three days of full moon each month, when they were unable to control their morphic stability.

Werwolfs were not human. Some of them were, once upon a time, but the vast majority – like Henrich, his wife, and their children – were born that way. They could pass for human most of the time, able to move between their human and wolf forms by sheer force of will. But when the great celestial orb was at its waxed apex and cast its ethereal blue light upon the earth, a werwolf's true form was revealed. They did not become savage, blood-thirsty beasts as some humans would have you believe, though Henrich did acknowledge the moon had something of an effect on his kind. They became... freer... less inhibited. More confident, certainly, and definitely stronger and more agile. And for some, like his late brother, they would become more aggressive. Hence, how some humans were turned into werwolf. Never on purpose. Always an accident, or in the throes of protecting oneself from a human aggressor. After all, all it took was a bite or a scratch. They always welcomed those newcomers to the pack and made a home for them, should they wish.

Humans had created all kinds of stories regarding the werwolf, even attributing mystical powers to them. You could not be turned by eating wolf meat, or being conceived under a full moon, or drinking water from a wolf's paw print, or consuming wolf's bane. And werwolfs were not invulnerable either, as the stories suggested, though they did heal very quickly. Yes, you could kill them with silver blades and arrows, or by removing their heads, though Henrich was fairly certain that would do for ending the life of most humans too. To him, it seemed a frivolously expensive way to dispose of another being.

"Do you think he will do as we ask?" said Hanna, nuzzling into him.

"What do you think?" snorted Henrich, putting his arm around her. "We must keep a close eye on him. I just hope the humans find whoever is responsible."

"Just one more night of full moon, my love," she soothed. "Then we are safe."

"Until next month," he replied, squeezing her shoulder.

***

September, AD 1802 – der Schwarzwald, near Hornberg, Baden. Third night of full moon.

Sebastien tracked the hunter through the forest's undergrowth, moving with cat-like grace, careful not to disturb an errant branch or make any sound that would draw the man's attention.

Shadows were not this quiet.

Seb grinned as he rounded the nearest tall, ancient pine and emerged on the other side, hidden from view by a heavy gorse thicket. He was merely a few feet away from the hunter now. So close that he could smell him: old leather, dead animals, stale sweat, and sour wine. And the hunter had no idea Sebastien was here.

In truth, the young werwolf had a close call two nights earlier. When he was sure his parents and sister were asleep, he had sneaked out, desperate to find a sign of the mysterious killer. Instead, he found the hunter. At first, Sebastien had assumed this man may have been the murderer, but the more he had watched the hunter, Sebastien realised that his first impression was incorrect. The murderer had brought his victims here – why would he be prowling in the dark in hope of finding another? Unless he too was tracking the real killer?

The man had turned sharply, firing his crossbow into the darkness on the clearing's other side. Had he found his quarry? Was it over already? Curiosity had gotten the better of Sebastien as he had peered through the bushes, edging closer to get a better look. In disappointed realisation, he saw the man's target was a simple squirrel, although the young werwolf admitted to more than a little admiration at the hunter's expert shot. At that moment, the man had spun and looked directly at Sebastien. The boy was frozen in terror, but only for a moment. Heart racing, he had gathered his wits, turned on his heel, and dashed into the forest's darkness. However, Sebastien had not gone home. Instead, he had waited in the darkness, then followed the hunter again, staying at a safe distance as the man traipsed through the Schwarzwald's periphery, setting traps of some kind. By the time Sebastien arrived home, the sun was cresting the horizon, turning the sky a dull blue/orange, and he had returned to his human form. He had crept into his family's cottage, slipped off his boots, and climbed into his bed still in his clothes. Moments later, he had heard his mother's footsteps, moving around the cottage's main living area, preparing breakfast.

"Where have you been?" his sister had hissed in their shared bedroom's dim light.

"Nowhere," he told her, sleepily.

The hunter had not even noticed Sebastien's presence on the second night, though the pup had kept his distance after the previous evening's narrow escape. But tonight? Tonight, the young werwolf was braver. Some would say reckless – certainly, the word his father would have used. Seb was fascinated by this man. He was taller than even his father, with greasy, long hair cascading beneath his felt jaeger hat. His clothes were shades of dark greens and browns, making him difficult to see to all but the keenest eyes – and werwolf night sight was exceptional. Many hunters wore blacks or dark blues, which made them stand out like a sore thumb in the woodland background. And this hunter did not smell like a human – his musk was more natural... more animal. Had Sebastien not been looking for him, he might never have discovered him. Or seen him coming. He gulped at that last thought.

"Sebastien Werner! What do you think you're doing?"

His heart leapt at the whispered chastisement, and he turned to find his sister, radiating disapproval. He frantically gestured to her to crouch, one finger to his lips, urging her to be silent. Despite her clear annoyance, Monika did as her brother asked and sidled close to him to peer out through the blanket of brambles. The hunter prowled on the other side, far too close for comfort.

Sebastien led his sister away, deeper into the forest where there was less risk of being overheard.

"What are you thinking, Seb?" Monika growled. "You saw those poor children. Do you want him to do the same to you?"

"You don't understand, Nika," Seb whispered. "I don't think he is the killer. I think he's hunting for the murderer too."

"Too? So, you're a hunter now, are you?" she mocked.

"No… I just… I want to help."

"You want to be nosey," she snapped. "You can't help yourself. The instant mother or father tell you *not* to do something, you do everything you can to break their rules. What if that man saw you? He's a hunter, Seb. He is *human*! Regardless of whether he's the murderer or not, he would still kill you."

Before Sebastien could reply, the crunch of a wayward foot crushing a branch made them turn. Through the trees approached a figure, a dark shape, hidden in the gloom. It paused, looking right at them. It appeared to be carrying something… something large… something heavy. Another noise came from their left, and the figure dumped its load on the ground, then turned and fled.

"Come on," hissed Seb and set off in pursuit.

"Sebastien! Stop!" cried Monika, as she followed after her brother.

As they passed, Seb caught sight of the stranger's cargo, discarded in the carpet of pine needles. It was a boy – a little older than Monika, he judged. He was pale, and groaning in pain, clutching at a puncture wound to his throat. Blood seeped between his fingers, as he eyed the werwolf siblings in equal parts afraid and beseeching their help. The puncture to his neck was not his only injury: one of the boy's wrists was bent at an unpleasant angle, and his face, throat, and arms were battered and bruised.

"Stay with him," ordered Seb, before continuing the chase.

The young werwolf was fleeter of foot than his larger quarry and he soon had the dark silhouette in sight again. Seb had his scent now… it was entirely human, masking its natural aroma with something sweeter, sharper.

Suddenly, the figure stumbled, crying out in pain – its fall accompanied by a sickening clang and crunch. They must have triggered one of the hunter's leg traps. As Sebastien drew near, it rose again and turned towards its pursuer. The young werwolf came to a skidding halt as the figure reached down and, with a grunt of effort, tore the iron jaws apart as though ripping the heel from a loaf of bread.

The figure took a step towards Sebastien and the werwolf boy swallowed hard. He froze, unable to flee. *What is this thing?* It was clearly no human. Eventually, Seb recovered control of his body. He turned and ran, heading away from this terrifying, pleasant-smelling creature. He had travelled only a short distance when an agonising, stabbing pain shot through his lower leg. He came to a shuddering stop as something bit at his ankle and he crashed to the forest floor, winding himself as he met the ground. He groped in the darkness, wincing as his fingers brushed the tortured mass of his shin, the trap's cold metal jaws of a trap, biting into his flesh. Fortunately, the leather of his thick riding boots had given his leg some protection, but the pain was visceral, and Sebastien could feel the bile rise in his stomach. He retched, expelling his supper over the mulch as he rocked back and forth, his nauseous mind swimming, unable to focus on anything other than his biting anguish.

"Seb!" cried Monika, running to his side. "Oh, my… are you okay?"

"Do I look okay?" he cried, tears running down his cheeks.

"What do I do? What do I do?"

But the pair were no longer alone. Emerging over the rise, came another figure. Advancing cautiously towards them. Seb's heart skipped a beat, but then he caught the scent. It was not his terrifying pursuer. This one stank of three-day-old sweat, musk, dirty hair, and fermented berries. It was the hunter.

"Go!" hissed Seb. "Get father!"

She shook her head in protest, clutching her brother's arms, but he pushed her away, and she finally ran for cover.

The hunter drew closer, and Sebastien could now make out details in the darkness. The man's long crossbow was braced against his shoulder, nocked, and levelled at him, ready to let fly should he make any sudden movements.

"Let me go," Seb cried out. "Please!"

"You can speak?" replied the hunter, lowering his crossbow.

"I was just thinking the same about you," Seb sneered, unable to restrain his sarcastic instincts.

"How many of you are there?" the man asked.

"There's just me," lied Seb, as another sharp twinge of agony shot up his leg.

"I saw at least one other."

"You are mistaken," Sebastien sobbed. "Please! This hurts so much! Let me go!"

"I can't. You've killed people."

"I have never killed anyone!" Seb screeched. "Rabbit, hare, deer – that is all. The occasional boar. My people stay away from humans."

"So, there *are* more of you?"

"No," Seb started, before realising there was no point in lying – the hunter had seen Monika. "Yes! Yes, of course there are. But I will never tell you where to find them. I would rather die!"

The hunter paused, seemingly torn, judging by the range of emotions vying for selection across his expressive features.

"We must have a culprit," he muttered, eventually.

"What?" asked Seb, in hollow realisation. "What do you mean?"

"Never mind."

The hunter stepped forward, straddling his feet on either side of the trap and gripped Seb by the shoulder. In panic, the young werwolf struggled to break free and sank his juvenile claws into the man's arm. Though not as strong as his father's, they were still sharp enough to penetrate the hunter's thick overcoat and underlayers, until they met flesh, piercing the skin. The man only winced, seemingly unfazed.

"Bloody hold still," he demanded, applying pressure to Seb's shoulder.

The hunter drew his knife and raised it aloft, where its blade caught the moon's light, reflecting its azure splendour. Seb shut his eyes, preparing himself for his painful end. The man tensed, and the young werwolf felt the rush of the blade heading towards him.

***

"Father!" cried Monika, shaking her dad into wakefulness.

"What is it, Nika?" he said, rousing from groggy reverie. On seeing his daughter's frantic expression, he snapped into sharp focus.

"What's going on?" asked Hanna, sitting bolt upright/.

"It's Sebastien," sobbed Monika. "The hunter got him."

"What?" cried Henrich, leaping from his bed and pulling on his pants. "Where?"

"I'll take you there," said Monika. Her father nodded and pulled his shirt on over his head.

"I'm coming too," said Hanna, grabbing her clothes.

"No, you stay here, Hanna," insisted Henrich.

"I wasn't asking permission," growled his wife. Henrich knew his wife's expression well enough not to argue.

***

Seb opened his eyes in puzzlement, to see the hunter prying open the trap's jaws. His blade was jammed into what must have been the release mechanism, enabling the trap to disengage. In relief, Seb pulled his leg free.

"Take off your boot," the hunter demanded.

"What?"

"Take off your damn boot, boy. Let's see what we're dealing with."

Seb did as he was ordered, unlacing the thick riding boot. He grimaced as the man stretched the bindings apart and yanked the boot free. He pushed Seb's pant leg up to take a closer look at the limb. It was red and swollen, with burgeoning bruises where the trap had clamped around his ankle.

"Hmmm… seems you have been lucky, my young friend," the hunter declared. "It's an old trap – the spring isn't what it once was. Doesn't seem to have broken the skin. Seems your boot took the brunt of it. Can you move it?"

Seb tentatively flexed his foot, wiggling his toes, and moving it up and down and from side to side, hissing through his teeth as he did.

"That's a good sign," said the man. "Now, on your feet – let's see if it can hold your weight."

He took Seb's hands and hoisted him upright, the werwolf boy balanced on one foot.

"Put your weight on it," insisted the man. "You planning to hop home?"

Wincing as he did, Seb slowly placed his foot down, feeling the sharp prickle of pine needles on his sole. He gradually shifted his weight onto his right foot, but a warning stab of pain forced him to lift it again.

The hunter eased Seb back down to the ground and knelt before him. He carefully took the pup's foot, rested it on his knee and brushed the needles from it. Then he reached into his pack and withdrew a roll of yellowing fabric.

"I don't think it's broken," he said, as he began to wind the fabric around the boy's injured ankle and foot. "It's going to be sore for a while. This should help you walk on it but take it easy for a few days at least."

"It's okay – we heal fast," Sebastien assured him.

Once the bandaging was complete, he helped the boy on with his boot, lacing it loosely and assisted him in climbing to his feet once more.

"How does that feel?" asked the hunter, his gruff tone belying the tender nature of his enquiry.

"Much better," replied Sebastien, testing his weight on the injured leg. It still hurt, but it was bearable. "Thank you."

"What's your name, boy?"

"Sebastien Werner, sir."

"Nice to meet you, Sebastien Werner. I'm Felix. I'm sorry you were caught in my trap. Now, what's a young boy like you doing out in the forest at night? Do your parents know you're here?"

Before Sebastien could respond, the pair were interrupted by the appearance of another figure.

"Step away from him, Seb," growled Henrich, his form silhouetted in a pool of moonlight. From here he looked taller and more imposing than usual – his claws flexed, ears pointed, eyes glistening like pearls in the darkness.

"It's okay, Father," insisted the werwolf boy, hobbling between his father and the hunter. "Felix is my friend. He won't hurt us."

"Nonsense!" roared Henrich. "That's all humans do. They kill and they take, and they don't give a damn about anything but themselves. Why is this one any different?"

"Because he could have killed me several times over already, but he hasn't," asserted Sebastien. "I stumbled into a trap, and he freed me, then he bandaged me up."

"That means nothing," snarled his father. "He could be the murderer for all you know. He stinks of death."

"No, Father," grinned the boy. "Felix just smells of body odour and dead rodents."

"Hey!" protested Felix.

"Besides," continued Sebastien, "I've seen the killer and it isn't him. I'm not even sure the killer *is* human."

"What? You've seen him?" gasped Felix, stepping forward. "Tell me, what did you see?"

"Stay back, hunter," warned Henrich, advancing on him.

"Stop it, Father," Sebastien implored, before turning back to Felix. The hunter crouched down so he was level with the young werwolf, though kept half an eye on the boy's father and a hand on his dagger's pommel.

"Please, Sebastien, tell me everything."

"I couldn't make out much," Seb told him. "He was shorter than you. Fatter too. And strong. He ripped apart your trap like it was paper."

"Yes, I saw what was left of it," grimaced Felix.

"And he smelled… nice… like… perfume?"

"Sandalwood and spice," mumbled Henrich. "I caught his scent last month."

At this, Felix' head snapped around, as though the mention of that particular scent was something familiar to him.

"And he was carrying a boy," continued Sebastien. "He dropped him when he saw Monika and me. Then he ran away."

"A boy?" asked Felix and Henrich, simultaneously.

With that, Monika appeared behind her father and whispered something to him.

"This way," said the werwolf father, gesturing to Felix to follow.

Monika led them through the woods to where her mother was attending to the boy. He was so pale now that his skin almost shone in the darkness.

"He's lost a lot of blood," Hanna told them. She was applying pressure to the wound, but the fabric was almost soaked red.

"Gustav?" exclaimed Felix, dropping to his knees at the boy's side. The boy was unconscious now, and his breathing was shallow and laboured.

"You know him?" asked Hanna.

"He is Gustav Dannecker," Felix explained. "His parents own the inn where I'm staying. The killer took their daughter last month. Will he live?"

Hanna looked to her husband, who shook his head in warning, then back to the hunter.

"I think it may be too late," she said. "He has lost too much blood."

Sebastien watched the exchange in incredulity, struggling to follow the conversation's unspoken subtext.

"What do you mean?" he asked, frowning. "We could—"

"No, Sebastien!" warned his father.

"What? I mean—"

"Sebastien!" barked Henrich, quieting the young boy at once.

He stood, head bowed in sullen silence. Was this it? Did they have to watch this poor boy die? A tear rolled down his cheek, and he absently wiped it away. To Sebastien's amazement, Monika took his hand in hers and squeezed it.

"We could always turn him," his sister suggested, shrugging in casual nonchalance.

Seb grinned, noticing with some amusement how his sister steadfastly avoided their father's furious glare.

The Watcher

"Turn him?" asked Felix. "You mean—?"

"Out of the question," said Henrich, flatly.

"Will it save him?" asked Felix, turning to Hanna.

"I... I don't know," she said. "It may be too late. But perhaps..."

"Hanna! We mustn't!" cried Henrich. "We agreed never to do this."

"Would you rather he died?" she said, glaring at her husband. "If he were our child and someone could help him, what would you have them do, Henri?"

Henrich sighed, his shoulders slumped. Seb smiled – he had seen this outcome so many times in his young life. For all his father was the uncompromising patriarch of their little family, his mother could tie him in logical knots when it really mattered, knowing precisely which levers to pull to appeal to her husband's good nature.

Henrich pushed Felix aside and knelt beside the boy, shaking his head, and muttering under his breath.

"Use the bite," Hanna said. "It's more certain."

Henrich nodded and lowered his head to the boy's slender shoulder. He opened his jaws wide and gently clamped them down, steadily applying pressure until his canines pierced Gustav's pale flesh. The boy moaned in his sleep and squirmed a little, though he remained unconscious.

"What now?" asked Felix.

"You have more bandages?" enquired Henrich.

"Yes."

"Then we patch him up and take him back to our home. If you're a religious man, hunter, I suggest you pray for the boy."

Despite Henrich's protests, with Hanna's consent – and prompted by the pleas of Sebastien and Monika – Felix was permitted to accompany the family of werwolfs back to their home. Felix was surprised to find they lived in a rather attractive, yet rustic cottage deeper in the forest, yet not too far away. According to Sebastien, this was one of many such dwellings hidden in the Schwarzwald. Felix was surprised he had never discovered one before.

He sat up all night with Gustav, his head lolling occasionally as he succumbed to oblivion. Each time his head slumped, the uncomfortable wooden chair would creak and shake him back to consciousness. The Werners had given the boy Sebastien's bed, and the young werwolf shared the neighbouring cot with his sister. As the pair slept, the rhythmic sound of their breathing became almost hypnotic, lulling Felix into Morpheus' warm embrace,

Around dawn, just as Felix began to drift off once more, Gustav's eyes opened. Felix snapped awake at once.

"Gustav? Are you okay?" he asked. The boy groaned and croaked, unable to form any words, but nodded. He was still pale and weak.

Felix dashed from the room, where he found a wooden jug of water. He poured a cup and carried it back to the boy, who took it, gratefully, and guzzled the lot in seconds. Felix poured him a second cup and helped him sit up, propping pillows behind Gustav's back. As the boy sipped the water, Felix unbandaged Gustav's neck wound to take a look at it. Amazingly, it appeared to have almost healed. The small, round lesion was still open, and the flesh around it pink and raw, though it was far healthier than Felix would have expected. The bruises around Gustav's neck and face had faded to yellow, whilst his badly broken right wrist did not seem to give the boy any pain, though it was still unnaturally crooked.

Gustav tried to speak once more, but the words would not come out, so Felix leaned in, straining to hear the boy's whisper. He spoke just one word. And Felix's eyes opened wide in shock as he registered what the Dannecker boy was trying to tell him.

*

"Are you leaving us?" asked Henrich, as Felix neatly restocked his pack. Hanna had graciously given him some dried meats and fruit, as well as replenishing his flask with water from their well. The Werner father's human form was far less fearsome than his werwolf appearance, Felix reflected. The man was of average height, with a slight build. His hair was yellow-blonde, whilst his eyes were the blue of sapphires. His clean-shaven features were lean and ruggedly handsome.

"Yes. I have something important to do."

"You know who the killer is?" enquired the werwolf.

"I think so. I'm not sure. However, I intend to find out."

"Then I wish you well, my friend," said Henrich, offering his hand. Felix hesitated for a moment, eyeing Werner with suspicion, but finally shook it.

"Please excuse my behaviour last night," offered Henrich, his cheeks flushing a little. "I was scared for my boy and the moon tends to make me a little more… gruff. That is no excuse. Thank you for helping Sebastien."

Felix nodded in acknowledgement. He was not one to hold grudges.

"What of the boy," he said. "He can never go home, can he?"

Henrich shook his head, sadly. "He can stay with us," he said. "We will make room. However, it is up to him. We can only explain the situation and hope he accepts it. I fear his parents will never understand."

Felix winced as he pulled on his heavy greatcoat and flexed his injured left arm.

"You are hurt?" enquired Henrich.

"Just a scratch," insisted Felix. "Your boy has quite a grip."

Henrich nodded, his expression set into an awkward grimace.

"You could always stay and have some breakfast with us before you go?" he offered. "I'm sure Seb would like to see you when he wakes."

"No, thank you. I have much to do. There is an errand I must attend to before I return to Hornberg."

"As you wish."

Felix shouldered his pack and crossbow, pulled on his hat, and headed for the door. He pulled it open but hesitated at the threshold.

"That's some boy you have there, Herr Werner," he said, smiling. "You must be very proud."

"Thank you," smiled Henrich. "You are welcome to visit Sebastien and Gustav any time, Felix. I just wish there were more humans like you."

Felix nodded. Then he closed the door behind him and headed out into the forest once more.

***

"Ah, do come in, Felix," said Friedrich from behind the ornate desk of his temporary office in the tavern's study. He stayed seated and gestured to the chair opposite. "Please, help yourself to schnapps or cheese. Or I can have Lina bring you something more substantial if you prefer?" He picked up the small silver bell from the desk's surface and held it, expectantly.

"No, thank you, Herr Markgraf Friedrich," said Felix. "I am very tired. This will not take long."

Felix did not have the patience to deal with these privileged men today – he had had three extremely long, punishing days and his temper was worn thin, not helped by the pain in his left arm. Though pain was not the right word for it – it was more a dull ache now. Like an itch he could not scratch. He had passed the distraught innkeepers on his way into the tavern, where Uli held his wife, Lina, as she sobbed. They had no idea what had become of their teenage son, but after Gretchen's murder the previous month, they could only fear the worst. It pained Felix that he could never tell them the truth.

That Friedrich had not acknowledged the Dannecker's pain meant he either did not know Gustav was missing, or he did know but did not give a damn. Felix knew which of those options he would put his money on.

Felix hefted the hessian sack then dropped it on the desktop before Friedrich. It made a solid thud as it landed, before falling to one side.

"You have found our culprit?" the markgraf asked, a faint smile playing across his lips.

"Oh yes, Herr Friedrich. I found him."

Friedrich opened the sack and peered inside.

"Is this it?" he said, seemingly disappointed. "It's a little small."

"That's your beast," Felix assured him. "A wolf. Just an ordinary wolf."

"It looks like a dog."

"It's a wolf, Herr Markgraf Friedrich. You wanted a culprit. I found one."

Friedrich paused, eyes narrowed, as though reading Felix' thoughts. Finally, he grinned, nodding in acceptance.

"Very good, Herr Schuster," he said. "Let me get your payment."

The markgraf rose from his seat and walked to the iron safe, walking with a noticeable limp. Friedrich opened the heavy door, then returned with a heavy leather satchel and placed it on the table between them.

"Three hundred gulden for three day's work, Herr Schuster, plus thirty thousand as reward for capturing our vicious beast." He gestured to the hessian sack. "Baden thanks you for your service."

Felix reached for the satchel, but Friedrich pulled it away a little.

"You're a rich man, Herr Schuster," grinned the markgraf. "Tell me, what do you plan to do with your newfound wealth?"

"I don't know Herr Markgraf Friedrich," shrugged Felix. "Maybe buy a little place to call home."

"An admirable thought, Herr Schuster. Schnapps?"

Friedrich limped to the office's other side and poured himself a large glass of the clear liquid.

"No, thank you," replied Felix. "You have hurt your leg?"

Friedrich sipped his schnapps and eyed the hunter again.

"It's nothing," he said. "just a flare-up of gout."

"Ah, that explains it," smiled Felix.

"There is a vacancy for a new freiherr in Hornberg, Herr Schuster," said Friedrich, rapidly changing the subject, "what with Herr Kuhl's sad passing – God rest his soul. I could use a good man at my right hand if you are interested? I can promise you generous compensation."

"Thank you, Herr Markgraf Friedrich," Felix replied. "However, I do not believe I would be a good fit for politics."

"Nonsense, man! You have a keen mind and sharp instincts – that is all you need. Aside from a haircut and a shave, of course, though that is easy enough. You would be a refreshing change from the usual toadying sycophants. But if you are sure?"

"Yes, I'm sure. I thank you for your generous offer."

Friedrich nodded, smiling warmly. "Well, if that is all, Herr Schuster, I must get on. I have a busy day ahead – and I must head home to Zähringen later today. Once more, I thank you for your service."

"Of course, Herr Markgraf," said Felix, hoisting the heavy satchel and rising from his seat. "Is there any news on Gustav?"

"Gustav?"

"The Dannecker boy? I heard he is missing?"

"Ah, of course, yes," said Friedrich. "Terrible business. To lose one child is bad enough, but two?"

"He is just missing, I believe?"

"Yes, yes, of course," agreed Friedrich. "Perhaps sneaked off to see a girl? You know what boys are like at that age. I have men searching the forest, nevertheless. We must have hope. Now, if you will excuse me, Herr Schuster?"

Felix nodded, never breaking eye contact with Friedrich. All the while, the markgraf maintained his glassy-eyed smile. Suddenly, Felix swung the satchel with all his strength, catching Friedrich full in the chest. The old man fell backwards into the occasional table, which collapsed under his weight as he crashed to the wooden floor in a heap of broken wood, shattered glass, and sticky alcohol.

"I know it was you!" roared Felix, dropping the satchel and drawing his hunting knife. "Unfortunately for you, Gustav survived. He *told* me what you did!"

He stepped over Friedrich's groaning form, brandishing the knife, threateningly. The old man lay there, eyes screwed shut, clutching at his chest. Felix grabbed him by the collar and hauled him up until the markgraf's face was just a few inches from his own.

"You're the murderer!" he hissed.

With that, Friedrich's eyes snapped open. But they had changed. Completely black. It was as though Felix was staring into the abyss. The aloof smile returned to the markgraf's lips as the old man drove his palm into Felix's chest, propelling him upwards with inhuman strength, until the hunter collided with the panelled ceiling. He fell to the ground, winded, gasping for air.

As he lay there, attempting to gather his wits, Felix heard running footsteps on the stairs and approaching the office door. It swung open and in charged Uli and Lina Dannecker, drawn to the sound of conflict.

"Oh, that is unfortunate," sighed Friedrich.

With a lazy waft of his left hand, the door slammed shut. Lina wrestled with the handle, but try as she might, it would not budge. Friedrich was upon them at once and Felix was helpless as the old man tore out Uli's throat with his bare hand, then snapped Lina's neck. The pair were dead in mere seconds.

Friedrich returned to Felix's prone form, grabbed him by the throat and lifted him, seemingly without effort, before slamming him against the wall.

"You should have taken the money and left, Herr Schuster," he said. "Then all this would have been over. You had a culprit. I could have walked away and found another means of satisfying my… proclivities. Such a waste."

Gasping for breath, the vice-like pressure of Friedrich's impossibly strong grip around his throat, Felix drove his hunting knife repeatedly into the markgraf's gut. Friedrich did not so much as flinch. He simply looked down at the knife – at Felix's blood-covered hand – and frowned.

"Really?" he said. "This was a bloody expensive waistcoat."

He threw Felix as if he were no more than a rag doll and he collided with the desk, slid across its surface, and came to rest in the fireplace's hearth.

The Watcher

"What... are... you?" Felix panted, clutching at his ribs. He feared they were broken.

Friedrich rounded the desk, pulled aside the office chair, and sat down on it, leaning over Felix.

"My dear boy," grinned the old man. "You could not possibly comprehend what I am." He blinked and, in an instant, his eyes reverted to their usual, pleasant hazel iris.

"If you are going to kill me, just get it over with," groaned the hunter.

"Kill you? Why would I do that? No, no, Herr Schuster. This works much better for me, actually. The people of the local villages hired a conman – a fraud – to track down their killer. A werwolf, indeed! It appears our hero – our knight in grubby armour – was the killer all along. He came back here, attempting to pass off this dog's head as our culprit and when I confronted him, he stabbed me and murdered the poor Danneckers before taking my money and making good his escape. Oh, I will make a full recovery from my injuries, of course, but I was powerless to stop one such as you. You are, after all, a werwolf."

"That won't work," sneered Felix. "I'll expose you."

"Who will the people believe, my boy?" grinned Friedrich. "A respected statesman such as I, or an itinerant, nomadic odd-job man?"

Felix was powerless to resist as Friedrich grabbed his left arm and inspected it.

"Besides," continued the markgraf, "judging by your injury here, I suspect my accusation is not a lie. And so, feel free to stay. By all means, put your fate in the hands of the people. That being said, I *will* have you thrown in a cell, where you will be held indefinitely. Oh, some people may doubt the veracity of my story – others may even believe your sorry tale. But when the next full moon rises, I suspect the people will be presented with irrefutable proof of my claims. However, you'll be stuck in a cell, with nowhere to go. Except to the executioner's block, of course. Meanwhile, I'll be miles from here, at home in Zähringen, recovering from my grave injuries."

Friedrich clasped Felix's hand and helped him to his feet.

"My advice is to take the money and run, Herr Schuster," offered the markgraf. "Better to be a wanted man than a dead man. Leave your knife, please. It will help support my claim – evidence, you know?"

He held out his hand, and Felix reluctantly handed him the dagger.

"The claw marks?" asked Felix, rubbing his sore ribs.

"Oh, that was a little on the nose, wasn't it?" grinned Friedrich. "Just a little evidential theatre – but a moment's effort with a penknife, dear boy. I always was a dab-hand at whittling. My father's carpenter taught me as a boy. Good times. I always knew it would come in useful one day."

With that, Friedrich led Felix to the door. He picked up the gulden-filled satchel as easily as if it were a cushion and handed it to the hunter. He opened the door, shoving Lina's body aside, and ushered Felix through it.

"Make haste, Herr Schuster," he warned. "I will give you a one-hour head start."

***

Minutes later, Felix and Walter were on the road again, heading north from Hornberg, towards Steinenbach. Felix shuddered as he recalled Friedrich's cold, black eyes. It was the darkness that lurked in the shadows. All fear lived in that place. Hope withered there. There was no light, no beauty, no courage – only dread and doom.

Just a mile along the road, Felix veered off the track and headed east, towards the Schwarzwald once more.

As usual, Walter became jittery and refused to move beyond the treeline, and so, with no little reluctance, Felix dismounted. He stripped his faithful companion of his bridle and saddle and stroked his muzzle with affection. Felix thanked Walter for their time together and, choking back his emotions, shooed the horse away. Walter hesitated, pawing the ground, but would not move.

Head bowed, unable to meet his old friend's eye, Felix slung the saddle over his shoulder and headed into the forest, never looking back. Walter would be okay – he was a fine horse, and someone was bound to take him in. If he were to look back, Felix would not be able to set him free.

Soon, he reached his destination. The day was unseasonably warm, and, with the extra weight of the saddle and the satchel of coins, Felix could feel the sweat running down his back and soaking through his clothes.

He dropped the saddle and unshouldered his pack containing all his worldly belongings. He paused, took a deep breath, and knocked on the door. It opened a moment later, revealing a short, blonde-haired grinning boy of about twelve years old.

"I knew it was you!" Sebastien cried, throwing his arms around the hunter's waist. "I could smell you coming for miles."

Henrich appeared at the door behind his son and nodded as one equal to another.

"Hello, Felix," he said. "We've been expecting you. I guess you have many questions? Please, come on in."

Felix accompanied the family of werwolfs into their home, and they closed the door, shutting out the vicious human world.

A Noble Heart Must Answer

October 1917, The Western Front, Ypres Salient, Belgium.

'*K*eep *the Home Fires Burning,*

While your hearts are yearning,

Though your lads are far away,

They dream of home…'

Sergeant Charlie Stepney inwardly groaned as he finished rolling his cigarette. He was so tired of this song now, but they were limited to just two surviving records after the previous week's heavy shelling. So, it was this or Elgar's frightfully dull 'Spirit of England' and he found that far too depressing. Personally, Charlie would have preferred a bit of peace and quiet, but this was what passed for entertainment in the trenches, and he could not deprive the men of that.

Charlie lit his cigarette and inhaled deeply. It was the one cigarette he allowed himself each day and, with tobacco rations running low, each smoke must be savoured. Especially as tonight he was picking up sentry duty, a task he hated. But

A Noble Heart Must Answer

Lieutenant Monteith had suggested it was good for moral that the non-commissioned officers be included in the rotation and Captain Bellingham had agreed. There was nothing Charlie could do about it and complaining would get him nowhere, so he knuckled down and got on with it. Plus, with their recent losses, it was decreed that sentry duty would be a solo task until reinforcements arrived. But Charlie had heard that tune for three years now — the promised fresh blood never seemed to reach his stretch of the line. It was all hands to the pump. After all, they were all in this together.

Despite high command's positive framing of the current war effort, the situation had escalated somewhat in recent months. Their lines were stretched, and each push saw devastating losses on both sides. Charlie felt certain their counterparts were in a similar state, so trying to pick a winner seemed rather arbitrary – at this point, it felt like the whole conflict could go either way. He had lost too many friends, seen too many terrible things to celebrate any perceived victory. His soul was numb... hollow... As a devout Christian, this Great War had shaken Charlie's faith, and he was not sure he could ever find that connection with God again. Not in the same way, at least. Even the thought of stepping into a church again was an uncomfortable thought.

A Noble Heart Must Answer

Charlie had tried to get his head down earlier that day, but the continuous rattle of artillery fire and the general hubbub of trench life made that impossible. Tonight promised to be long and tedious, but he plucked the watch, his father's old brass one, from the pocket of his heavy tunic and checked it. Before pocketing it again, he flicked open the concealed section in the case front and stared, wistfully, at the small photograph within. Then he clicked the case closed and with a practised, skilled hand, let the watch slip from his fingers, caught the heavy chain and swung it around until he clasped it in his palm and slipped it back into his pocket in a single movement. They had a lot of time in the trenches and very little to occupy their minds, so Charlie had perfected this slick routine within a few weeks of arriving at the front. He did it without thinking now, though it still drew admiring applause from the young lads new to the trenches.

"Five more minutes, then switch that racket off, lads," Charlie said, poking his head inside the pokey quarters shared by Privates Albert Dawkins and Reginald Williams. Those were the rules on the front-line trenches: lights were only permitted in covered quarters, not out in the open, and no noise was allowed after dark. Nothing that Jerry could use to target their lines.

"No probs, Sarge," said Albert. "You on watch tonight?" Albie was a pleasant, affable fella – popular with all the men and always ready with a joke or bawdy tale to keep up morale. He was actually from the same Berkshire town as Charlie and only a year his junior, though the pair had only met in this very trench.

"Yes, I have that dubious pleasure, Albie," groaned Charlie.

"Well, look out for the Woman in White," warned Albert, his voice filled with mock sincerity.

"Oi, leave it out!" moaned Reggie. "She's real, I tell you. Seen her wiv me own eyes."

"Yeah, yeah, course she is," chuckled Albert.

"Sarge! Tell 'im!" whined Reggie.

"Oh, come on, Reg," jibed Albie. "It's a load of old bollocks."

"'Tis not!" insisted Reggie. "She's real! I'm not on me own, neither. Some o' the other lads 'ave seen her too."

"Okay, calm it down, you two," chided Charlie.

"Evening chaps. What are we talking about?"

Charlie jumped to his feet and saluted as Lieutenant Donald Monteith appeared, smiling affably. Both privates followed suit.

"At ease, chaps," said Monteith. "It's only me."

Monteith was one of the more popular officers amongst the trench rank and file, being generally warm-natured and pleasant, though with a sharp wit that enabled him to hold his own with the best of them. He was popular despite having little common ground with the soldiers, coming from an affluent, upper-class family and having been taught in the most exclusive public schools. Monteith was Scottish, but his accent was so plummy you would never guess – he sounded more English than even the poshest of English boys. Even Charlie liked him, and he hated most all of the officers.

"Ah, Private Williams was just regaling us with a popular ghost story, Lieutenant," Charlie told him. "His attempt to tease me ahead of sentry duty, I believe."

"Ghost story?" grinned Monteith. "I do love a good spooky tale. Please, do tell, Private Williams."

Reggie's eyes darted to Charlie, seeking permission from his sergeant. Charlie sighed but nodded.

"Okay, well, Lieutenant… have you heard of the Woman in White, sir?"

"The Woman in White?" smiled Monteith, taking a seat in the quarters and helping himself to a grimy tin cup of the dreadful scotch Charlie's brother had sent him last Christmas, but had taken so long to arrive that the following festive period was almost upon them. "No, I've not heard of her, Private. Please enlighten me."

"Right, well, fing is," said Reggie, clearing his throat and settling into his story-telling patter. "The Woman in White is a lost soul, her spirit cursed to wander the earth, seeking out violent men to punish for their 'orrible ways. See, this woman was murdered by 'er husband, so she is bent on avenging 'er own death. As soldiers, we're fair game, see? None more violent than us. Death is all around us. But if you see the Woman in White, she beguiles you with her beauty, lures you away, and steals your very soul. Even if you don't go wiv 'er, misfortune awaits. If you see her, you're doomed! She's a 'arpbinjer."

Monteith snorted, almost spitting out the foul whiskey. "Do you mean 'harbinger', Private Williams?"

"Yeah, one o' them fings, sir. Binjin' all over the gaff."

"'Ere, 'ang on a bloody minute," scoffed Albert. "You said anyone who sees her is doomed. You told me you seen her yourself, you fool!"

"Yeah, an' that was true," said Reggie. "Who knows what fate awaits me now? Alls I know is, I haven't slept a night right through since I saw her. She haunts my dreams. I'm scared to go to sleep in case I don't wake up again. Any day might be my last."

The quarters fell silent, and Reggie's expression was so haunted that Charlie actually started to believe his story, but only for a moment. The spell was broken by Albert, bursting out with a bark of laughter.

"Oh, shut up, you pillock!" he chortled. "You almost bloody 'ad me there, you plank."

Reggie's expression was scandalised, filled with bottled fury, his cheeks reddening, and lip curled into a snarl. But after a moment, he broke into a huge grin and laughed, slapping his knee.

"I know, I know," he laughed. "Couldn't keep me face straight. But the look on your boat[1], Sarge."

---

[1] Cockney rhyming slang: Boat = Boat Race = Face.

"Yeah, yeah," huffed Charlie. "Right, bed down, you pair. Switch off that bloody gramophone, dim the lights and keep it down, eh?"

"Yes, Sarge," saluted Reggie.

"Oh, while I fink on, Sarge," said Albie. He handed Charlie a Thermos in one hand and, with the other, a bar of Fry's Chocolate Cream. "Coffee and a bit of a sweet treat for while you're on duty tonight."

"Is this from your rations, Albie?" asked Charlie. "You don't need to do that."

"It's okay, Sarge. You're muckin' in with the rest of the lads on watch, so it's the least I can do."

Charlie looked to Monteith, who just smiled, knowingly.

"Well, thank you, Albie," said Charlie. "That's very good of you."

"Don't mention it, Sarge. Just look out for the Woman in White. Wooooo!"

"Oh, give over, will you?" moaned Reggie, as Charlie and Lieutenant Monteith exited the quarters and pulled the heavy fabric curtain back across the narrow doorway.

A Noble Heart Must Answer

"You see?" said Monteith as the pair strolled along the duckboards that lined the trench floor. "The men see you as one of them, Sergeant Stepney. In these troubled times, it's important they feel a connection to their officers. You can offer that in a way I never could. You're a good leader, Charlie."

"Thank you, sir."

"It's more important now than ever, Sergeant. These past months have been hard on us all. But there is more to come. I sense another push will be ordered any day now."

"Really sir?" said Charlie. "We're still waiting on reinforcements to replace our losses from the last push."

"I am aware, Sergeant. Unfortunately, I do not give the orders. Just be ready, should it come to that. I believe the war is delicately balanced, and we will have an important part to play in assuring victory. Stay vigilant, Sergeant. Keep the men's spirits up. We're close to the end now – I can feel it."

"Yes, sir. Thank you, sir," said Charlie, dutifully, though he doubted Monteith's words. The past three years weighed heavy on his soul, and the end appeared no closer than it had that first Christmas. Home had never felt so far away – as though even to dream of returning was foolish.

"Good man," grinned Monteith, saluting. "Carry on."

The lieutenant turned and headed back towards the interconnecting communications trench that led to his own quarters away from the front-line trench. He stopped before he turned the corner and turned back to face Charlie, a mischievous twinkle in his eye.

"Oh, and Charlie?"

"Yes, sir?"

"Do keep your eyes peeled for the Woman in White, eh?"

He turned the corner, chuckling, and disappeared from view.

***

Charlie stretched, yawned expansively, and rubbed at his exhausted eyes. The chocolate was long gone, and his stomach rumbled with hunger, whilst his leg twitched, irritably. He took out his father's pocket watch, flipped it open, then balanced it in a recess in the trench wall. He took out his brass cigarette lighter, fashioned by one of the men from a bullet casing and, cupping his hands over it to shield the light, struck the flint. After a few attempts, the flame sprung to life, just for a moment, illuminating the pocket watch and filling Charlie's nostrils with the warm, sweet aroma of petrol. Just after oh-three-hundred-hours and all was... well... dull. Just how Charlie liked it. Excitement in the trenches tended to coincide with copious amounts of death and destruction. Boredom was a soldier's best friend.

Still, four more hours of watch to go before Charlie could get his head down. He clambered up the trench wall again, took his field glasses from their leather case and, poking his head just above the stacked sandbags that formed the parapet, peered out over No-Man's Land. He adjusted the focus, not that it made much difference. There was little to see in the pitch darkness. All Charlie could hope for was to see any shadows or shapes moving through the dark.

In truth, the likelihood of catching sight of any German spies reconnoitring allied lines was slim, let alone being able to open fire upon them with any degree of accuracy. Any soldier brave or foolhardy enough to venture into No-Man's Land was more likely to meet their end from one of the many landmines that littered the plane as from an enemy bullet. Charlie had sent many men to their doom on one of these largely fruitless reconnaissance missions. Those that returned quite often came back with little information of any significant value. But still, orders were orders.

Charlie slid down the trench wall, stuffed his field glasses back into their snugly fitting leather case and refastened the clasp. Then he took out the flask and poured the last, lukewarm dregs into the cap then downed it. The French coffee was bitter and unpleasant. It used to be vaguely drinkable with sugar and milk, but those rations had long since run out, so now it was simply tolerated for its caffeinating qualities. The flavour alone was enough to rattle the most somnambulant senses into juddering wakefulness.

As he screwed the flask's cap in place, the sudden introduction of an alien, yet familiar, noise shook Charlie into wide-eyed focus. Music drifted along the trench, cutting through the silence like nails down a blackboard. He jumped to his feet and, following the sound, ran along the duckboards until he reached Albie and Reggie's quarters. He burst through the curtain, finding both men curled up on their bunks, their backs to him. The gramophone's turntable whirred away, the record spinning around and around, the stylus of the tone arm reading the album's grooves, reproducing the scratchy sound of *Keep the Home Fires Burning* and piercing the night's silence with all the subtlety of a rocket flare. Charlie snatched the tone arm and angrily dragged it across the record, with an abrupt, squealing scratch.

"What the devil do you think you're doing?" he demanded.

Both privates jumped awake, seeming oblivious to the blaring music of a few seconds earlier.

"Sarge?" groaned Albie, squinting. "What's goin' on?"

"You tell me?" hissed Charlie. "Is this your idea of a joke? Well, I don't find it amusing in the slightest."

"What you on about, Sarge?" asked Reggie.

"The blasted music?" snarled Charlie. "Booming out at full volume, putting a bloody target on your backs? Are you bloody stupid?"

"What music, Sarge?" protested Albie. "I don't know what you're on about, honest."

Charlie growled and snatched the record off the gramophone. "Well done, chaps," he snapped. "You've just gone and lost your music privileges. Now get to sleep and no more sodding around, do you hear me?"

Charlie stormed out into the trench and, in a fit of instantly regretted pique, lashed the vinyl disc into No-Man's

Land. Perhaps he was a little hasty, he chided himself. After all, entertainment was hard to come by in the trenches, so the men would often play daft tricks on each other for fun and as a minor distraction from the horrors that overwhelmed their every day. No! There were limits. All it took was one uncovered lamp, or a single, overly raised voice and the Jerries would use you for artillery target practice. Cursing his affability, Charlie returned to his post.

Minutes felt like hours on solo sentry duty, and it was all Charlie could do to keep from slipping into unconsciousness. He rubbed his eyes and inhaled deeply, stifling a yawn. But then it came again. Music! The same bloody song! Keep the Home Fires Burning... but how? Oh, how Charlie had grown to hate that damned song.

With a snarl of fury, he stormed along the trench again and whipped open the curtain to Albie and Reggie's quarters once more. The music ceased the moment he did.

Heart pounding and blood rushing in his ears, Charlie caught his breath and attempted to make sense of what was happening.

The gramophone's turntable was empty, devoid of any record, let alone the one he himself had disposed of just a short while earlier. But he had *heard* it. He was *sure*. Or was he? Could he have dreamt it? Had he fallen asleep and imagined the whole thing? Was it a hallucination brought on by sheer exhaustion?

"Sarge?" grumbled Reggie, rolling over in his bunk. "Everyfink okay?"

"Go back to sleep, Reggie. Everything's fine."

Confused and discombobulated, Charlie stepped outside again and took another deep breath. He shook his head, chastising himself for falling asleep on duty. He must stay standing for the rest of the night. And then – off to his right, further along the trench – a sudden movement, gone as soon as he looked at it. Something white.

The trenches did not run in straight lines. Instead, they were carved into the ground in zigzag lines, meaning one could only see about twenty feet in any direction before the wall curved away, obliterating your view. Charlie moved towards the unseen object, treading carefully over the swollen, semi-rotten boards. Was he seeing things now? He turned the corner and there she was, just rounding the turn ahead of him. A woman, clad in a long, white dress, with dark hair that cascaded over her shoulders. She seemed to glow from within, casting her light over the midnight trench. Charlie hurried after her, heart pounding, the duckboards flexing and shifting treacherously beneath his feet. Another turn, then another, then another, the Woman in White turning the corner each time he rounded his. But then, at the next turn, there she was. Charlie stopped in his tracks. She stood in the centre of the trench, staring at him with piercing, dark eyes, an amused expression on her pale features, head tilted to one side and a wan smile splayed across her soft, heart-shaped lips. She must have been no older than mid-twenties. Attractive, yet exuding a sadness that belied her youthful appearance. The woman was slightly translucent, and Charlie could just make out the shape of the ladder behind her, perched against the trench wall.

She extended her arm and beckoned to Charlie. Overcoming his instinct to turn and run, he took a deep breath and took a step towards her. His feet were heavy as lead as he lifted each one in turn and, his breath escaping in short, staccato bursts, made the short, trepidatious journey towards the spectre. Charlie stopped just an arm's length away. From here, the woman was truly beautiful, yet radiated an ineffable sorrow. And she looked so familiar. She smiled, softly, pleasantly, lovingly, and Charlie felt no malice from her. After three years of people trying to kill him every day, Charlie knew spite when he saw it. She seemed to glow in the trench's gloom, though the light she emitted was chillier than even the early winter night of West Flanders.

"Who…?" Charlie began, but the Woman in White raised a finger to her lips to silence him. She raised her eyes to the sky, squinting slightly, eyes flitting, and head cocked slightly, as though listening for something.

"What is it?" hissed Charlie. "What are you trying to tell me? I don't understand."

The Woman in White locked eyes with him again, frowning. She opened her mouth to speak, but no words came out. Charlie could see her lips moving, but there was no sound. He shook his head, not understanding, and the woman flailed her arms in exasperation, balling her hands into fists, teeth gritted. Finally, she seemed to gather her composure, raised her open palms, closed her eyes, serenely, inhaled, and respired through pursed lips in an apparent show of frustration. She locked eyes with Charlie, then opened her mouth again. This time, she did not try to speak but Charlie heard something, quite clearly. It was a song:

'Keep the Home Fires Burning,

While your hearts are yearning…'

Charlie blinked, shocked. It was the sound of a gramophone record, as though coming from a great distance.

'Though your lads are far away,

They dream of home…'

Her mouth snapped shut and the song abruptly stopped. And this time, the words she mouthed were clear to Charlie.

"Get down!"

Eyes widening in sudden realisation, he threw himself forward, crashing onto the sodden duckboards as the world behind him erupted in a chaotic, deafening tumult of searing heat, and blinding light that scarred itself onto his retinas even with his eyes tightly screwed shut. And it went on and on for an eternity.

***

Seventeen men perished in the shelling, including Reggie and Albie. Charlie and dozens of others spent the morning picking through the wreckage of collapsed quarters, extracting the bodies and… parts thereof. After the horrors of the previous three years, Charlie was numb to even the most stomach-churning barbarities. And yet, the close call that almost saw him become this tragedy's eighteenth victim chilled him to his core. And yet, he did his bit, ashen-faced, trembling, pulling arms, legs, and unidentifiable innards from the earth and placing them into canvas sacks. The rain fell, drenching him through his clothes. His boots squelched as he moved, whilst his icy cold fingers felt as though they belonged to someone else. And yet, he would not retire, in the very slim hope they would find one of his charges – his *friends* – still alive in the rubble. But after four hours, Monteith called off the recovery efforts. They shut down the destroyed line of trench – even the surviving structures were too unstable to be occupied.

Of course, Charlie did not mention the Woman in White during his debrief. The last thing he needed was to be locked-up in a psychiatric hospital.

***

As Charlie had predicted, the conflict on the Western Front heightened as winter set in. The expected tip in the Allies' favour – as French and American reinforcements joined the fray in Ypres and other key battlegrounds – never materialised.

A Noble Heart Must Answer

The additional soldiers failed to prove themselves in the field – sheer numbers of men were simply not enough. By spring of 1918, the German assault had forced the Allies into a retreat, their resources severely weakened by disastrous offensive after disastrous offensive. Charlie felt like a husk of the man he was before, his faith all-but dissolved, replaced by a grim, almost nihilistic resolve to survive. By summer, the tide turned again, and the Allies launched a fierce counter-offensive – at last, the Yanks and the Frenchies came good. In each battle, as Charlie inspected the faces of the men fighting at his side, he saw the same look of exhausted, haunted, resolve. It was as though they were dead men already, their bodies still animated, fighting this war to the finish for the loved ones they left behind. And as soon as it is over, they would lie down and go to their rest.

On November 11th, the armistice was signed, bringing a welcome end to the slaughter, and Charlie Stepney could finally return home – though he always felt as though a part of him remained in Ypres. Even when he met Madeleine. Even when they married. Even when their daughter, Emily, arrived. Oh, he was content enough. Happy, even. But civilian life felt as though the brightness was turned down. As though the sound was muted, just like the Woman in White's voice. That moment would frequently come back to Charlie, often unbidden, in those quiet moments when his mind would drift; in his office at the Prudential, or when mowing the lawn, or sat sipping a glass of single malt by the fire in their front room. The country was getting back on its feet after the devastation of the Great War, and Charlie was doing his part, rebuilding his life, raising his daughter, being a good husband, contributing to society, and fighting back the demons that promised to drag his soul to hell for all the terrible things he did during wartime, all in the name of freedom.

He often thought he saw the Woman in White – just from the corner of his eye, or in his reflection, or through the bottom of a tumbler of scotch. But Charlie simply put that down to a remnant memory from his deeply scarred psyche.

***

"He's gone, Missus Downing," the doctor told her, checking Charlie Stepney's pulse for the final time. "I'm very sorry for your loss."

Emily wiped the tears from her eyes and nodded, offering her lip-trembling thanks to the doctor and nurses who cared for her father in his final days. She had known the end was coming for months, but it made it no easier now that he had slipped away. She was still reeling from her mother's sudden death a year earlier. After that, Dad just seemed to give up. He had always been a quiet, reserved man, somewhat lost in his thoughts – a troubled soul. Mum just said he had been that way for as long as she had known him. She said many of the boys who came home from the war were just the same. Just as burdened and damaged by their experiences. Emily saw the same despondency in her husband, Trevor, when he had returned from WWII a decade earlier.

But, in truth, her father's passing was a kindness. Cancer had ravaged his body for five long years, but he never complained. Never made a fuss. But once Mum was gone, it was as though his will to fight died with her. It was cruel just how much this wonderful man had endured in his sixty-eight years on this earth.

Charlie Stepney was gone, but he was finally at peace.

***

A Noble Heart Must Answer

"Mum, what's this?" asked Michael.

Emily put down the box of her father's old clothes in the hallway and entered her father's dusty old study, where she found her ten-year-old son inspecting a crumbing shoe box.

"Photographs," she said, taking the box from him and riffling through the contents. "Grandad when he was a young man, during the war. And letters from home, I'm guessing." She smiled at the sight of her young dad in the pictures, in better times, before the permanent sadness had affixed itself to his soul. He looked happy, with a broad, ready grin, filled with mischief and good humour. She lifted the stack of crisply folded, yellowing papers and sepia photographs from the box, revealing another object, hidden beneath.

"Is it gold?" gasped Michael, lifting the metal disc from its home and turning it over in avaricious fingers. "What is it?"

"It's a pocket watch, Michael," Emily told him, ruffling his hair. "More likely brass than gold, I expect."

"How does it work?"

"I don't think it does."

Emily took the timepiece from her son and inspected it. She clicked the clasp latch on the case's side, and it popped open, revealing the watch bezel and its white face beneath, the Roman numerals exquisitely hand-painted beneath. The hands had been frozen in time for decades.

"I remember this," she muttered, and popped the second, hidden latch between the case front and the watch, revealing a small, hinged disc. Enclosed beneath the glass was a faded photograph of a woman holding a swaddled baby.

"Who's that?" asked Michael, peering over his mother's shoulder.

"Well, that baby is your grandad," she told him. "And the woman, I believe is his mother – your great-grandmother, Iris."

"I didn't know I had a great-grandmother."

"I never met her either, darling," sighed Emily. "Grandad didn't talk about her much. She died when he was just a boy, apparently."

She handed the watch to Michael so he could take a closer look.

"She's really pretty," he said. "She looks just like you, mum."

"Do you think?" smiled Emily. "I never really noticed before."

She peered at the image again, of the attractive young woman with the dark curls, wearing her pristine white dress, and clutching her child with such pride, such adoration in her eyes. Emily could not contemplate how terrible it must have been for her father to lose this woman before he ever really knew her. And for Iris to have known she was going to be ripped from his life, to never see him grow into the wonderful man he became. Emily was not sure she could cope with such loss. She could not bear the thought of being taken from Michael. She would move heaven and earth to prevent that from happening. Emily was not religious — her father had no place in his heart for the church after his experiences in the Great War, and that had rubbed off on her. Emily did not know if there was any such thing as an afterlife but, if there was anything beyond this plane of existence, it could not keep her from her son.

"You should have it," she told Michael. "It was your grandad's, and his father's before. It's an heirloom."

"Thanks, Mum! Are you sure?"

"Yes, he would want you to have it."

"Thank you!" he squealed, grasping the watch, and dashing from the room to show his father.

"No running in the house!" Emily called after him, smiling and shaking her head. As she turned to leave, she caught her reflection in the mirror and gasped. In the image, behind her, was a woman, dressed all in white. She spun around but the woman was nowhere to be seen, but when she turned back to the mirror, there she was. The woman had a gentle, pleasant smile affixed to her heart-shaped lips, with dark curls cascading to her shoulders. Emily realised she was holding her breath, her heart racing, and head swimming in panic. She exhaled, gathered her composure, and swallowed hard. There was no reason to be afraid. This woman was no threat to her or her family. She just wanted Emily to know she was there. The woman smiled, as one mother to another. And then she was gone, disappearing in the blink of an eye, as though she was never there.

Michael had been right: Emily did look just like her.

Forlorn

September, AD 2021, Woodchester Mansion, nr Nympsfield, Gloucester, UK.

Woodchester Mansion has lain abandoned for over a hundred-and-forty years. Unlike most derelict stately homes, this one was a little different. It was never *home* to anyone. No people raised families here, no loving partners grew old here, furnishing the lavish rooms with their memories, both good and bad.

The dilapidated, partially completed manor fell into disrepair, only rescued by the trust established to renovate the old house and open it up to visitors, thus enabling others to witness this beautiful building, with its sumptuous stonework and elegant carvings. Though as stunning as this wonderful stately home was, few could spend much time there. Rumours abounded that the old place was haunted, though there were no records that anyone had ever died at Woodchester, aside from vague anecdotes that a French plasterer was bludgeoned to death shortly before the owner went bankrupt in the late nineteenth century. The project had ground to a halt as the bank seized the property, and the house had remained empty ever since.

When you enter most old houses, you can feel the love of the residents who called it home. Their ardour permeates the brickwork, the wood, the plaster, and radiates from it, to be absorbed by all who visit. The same feeling could be experienced at Woodchester, which is odd for a building in which nobody had ever lived.

Until you start to think about why that might be.

︿

The crunch of splintering wood alerted Beatrix that someone was coming. Someone was entering the house. No one came at night. But then, no one came here at all lately.

Unable to contain her excitement, she rushed along the landing and down the ornate stairwell until she had sight of the entrance hall. She crouched down peering through the beautifully carved limestone columns that separated the stairwell from the foyer, just as the unknown visitors levered open the door until it was just wide enough to squeeze through. Three of them slipped in, mere shapeless shadows of darker black in the midnight gloom. Once inside, each of the three ignited their handheld electric lamps – torches, Beatrix had heard them called before – and cast their beams around the open space. One momentarily settled upon Beatrix's hiding place and she flinched and cowered away from the light, though she had no idea why. They would not see her. Nobody ever saw her.

"This way," hissed the trio's leader, beckoning the others through the archway to the left and into the space beyond. Beatrix followed, moving swiftly, yet carefully, keeping the intruders in view.

"Why are we whispering, Smithy?" asked one of them, the smallest of the three.

"I… honestly, I've no idea, Meg," chuckled the leader.

"You sure there's no-one here?" asked the third prowler.

"Yeah, I'm sure of it, Gav," assured the one called Smithy. "All our lads were taken off-site for the foreseeable. No tours going on and the renovations have stopped until April next year at the earliest. We've put in cameras, but I can control them from my phone. There's only me and two other lads checking the feeds and I've paid them to turn a blind eye."

"Perfect, Smithy," said Gav. "We can set up here for the next few months."

"Yeah, just need to bring in a diesel gennie," confirmed Smithy. "How quickly can your lads get the lab set up, Meg?"

The one they called Meg stepped away from the others and wandered around the space, appraising it. Beatrix watched her, intrigued. She had never seen a girl like her before, with piercings in her nostril and eyebrow, as well as several in each ear. Her hair was shaved at the sides, with the short crop of lank hair on top dyed a vivid green. She had some form of artwork stencilled on the skin of her neck and hands, though Beatrix could not see the details from here.

"Dust could be a problem," the girl said. "We'll need a couple of serious HEPA filters and some good-sized plastic tenting. That fireplace work or is it blocked up?"

"I think it works," shrugged Smithy. "Not checked."

"Well, get it checked," demanded Meg. "We'll need to vent somewhere. The chimney will do the job nicely – otherwise, that could be a problem."

"Okay, babes, I'll get it checked out."

"I'm not your babes, you fat prick," she scowled, before storming into the neighbouring room.

"Fucking hell, don't wind her up, Smithy," hissed Gav.

"Oh, she loves it really."

Beatrix had already crept past the two men, following Meg as she continued her exploration of the derelict manor. She caught up as the girl slipped through a doorway and into one of the ground floor's few partially furnished rooms; the drawing room at the property's rear, with large windows overlooking the gardens.

Meg wandered over to the exquisite fireplace, brushing her finger over the mantlepiece, and stared into the massive, giltwood-framed mirror mounted above it. She smiled, running her fingers through her hair. And then she stopped, her smile fading, eyes wide as she stared past her reflection to the semi-translucent image over her left shoulder.

"Hello," said Beatrix, offering Meg a timid wave.

Meg spun around, her breaths coming in rapid bursts, feet frozen to the spot.

"You can see me?" asked Beatrix.

Meg suddenly gained control of her legs. And her lungs. She screamed and sprinted for the doorway, barrelling through it as fast as she could, without looking back.

"What's going on?" demanded Smithy as he and Gav followed the fleeing Meg out into the driveway.

"Fucked if I know, mate," shrugged Gav. "You sure there's no security here?"

"Nah, mate. Let's just get in the van though, eh? Just in case."

Beatrix could only watch, downcast and miserable as their voices faded away. She heard the rumble of their vehicle's engine as they tore away across the gravel drive, heading for the exit. She sighed, resignedly.

She was alone. Again.

*

It was the solitude that Beatrix found most difficult. She had no concept of how long she had been alone here. Decades? Perhaps even longer? The days were interminably long when you no longer required sleep – they all blended together after a while.

Beatrix had seen much change since she first came to be here, though the building was still little more complete than when she first arrived. What year was that? 1873 seemed to ring a bell, but she could no longer be sure. But then, she had no concept of what year it was now. How old had she been? Twenty-four? Twenty-five? She may have been married. There was a phantom gold band on her wedding finger, certainly, though she had no recollection of a husband at all. She struggled to recall much about the time before.

There was still so much confusion about how she came to be here. Woodchester Mansion was not her home when she was alive – of that much she was certain – but now she was stuck in this place. She could no more leave than she could feel the cold. Oh, Beatrix was perfectly aware she was dead. She could not quite remember *how* it had happened. She came to Woodchester, she recalled, and met with the man who owned the place... what was his name? Bob? Bill? Something like that. He had seemed nice enough, she recalled, in a desperate kind of way. He had become very unhappy with her, though. She remembered a sudden, sharp pain to the back of her head, then nothing. Darkness.

There were times when she could vaguely recall meeting... someone... someone else. Not here. It was... elsewhere. He wanted her to go with him. But Beatrix was scared. She ran away. Or at least she thinks she did. All she knows is the next thing she could recall was finding herself back in the semi-finished mansion, alone, unable to feel, to touch, to be seen. At least, not by most people it seemed.

When the renovations restarted, Beatrix felt more at home. She found comfort in the company of workmen, even though they were unaware of her presence. And the tours were nice too. She liked hearing about the building's history, but more so about the fleeting minutiae of the numerous visitors. She could pretend she was one of them, able to mingle, listen to their conversations and even their petty arguments. It made her feel alive.

For a time, the house had a caretaker living on site. Andy, was it? Beatrix liked Andy and found him pleasant company. He never saw her or communicated with her, though he sometimes seemed aware she was there, which Beatrix found comforting. Andy moved on a long time ago, replaced by sporadic, uniformed security officers, though they never spent much time inside the building. They all seemed to rush away as soon as they could.

Lately, the tours had ceased, and even the security guards' visits were increasingly infrequent.

At least she still had the bats for company. Beatrix *loved* the bats that occupied the attic. They were sweet and pleasant, and she was certain they could sense her. She talked to them most evenings when they returned from their hunt and before they settled down to roost. She would love to hold them, to stroke them, if only she could feel... well... anything.

Once more, Beatrix was alone.

***

Time passed, as it was wont to do. Beatrix had little concept of how much had gone by since her last visitors, though the days had grown short, and a film of frost had begun to form on the windows each night.

It looked a brittle, cold morning, whilst the heavy, grey clouds threatened rain. Beatrix remembered that feeling – the pressure, the tension in the air, the tang of humidity. She always loved the rain. The susurration as it swept through the trees, drumming on the roof and windows, bouncing off the pavements and puddles. She longed to run outside, to immerse herself in the falling droplets. For them to soak through her clothes as she turned her face to the heavens and gloried in the blissful cascade. But she could no more do that than she could lift the claw hammer which sat propped against the nearby wall. It was as if there was an invisible barrier at each exit – even if the doors were left open, she could not pass through them. She was trapped here. Forever.

That's not to say Beatrix did not love Woodchester. She did, with every fibre of her being, but she was so very lonely.

"Hello?"

The sound of an unknown voice shook Beatrix from her sullen reverie. She sat upright and listened, waiting for the newcomer to speak again. Had she imagined it? Had she finally lost her mind through miserable solitude?

They spoke again.

"Hello? Is anyone there?"

A woman's voice. Young, softly spoken. Beatrix dashed along the landing and down the stairwell to her partially obscured vantage point overlooking the entrance hall. Sure enough, there was a woman, wrapped in a heavy coat with, scarf, gloves and a matching woollen hat. The front door still stood slightly ajar from the previous prowlers, and brown, gold, and burnished red leaves were scattered across the floor.

The woman looked up, staring directly at Beatrix, so she ducked away, hiding behind the nearest pillar.

"Oh, hi," the woman said, cheerfully. "It's okay – I won't hurt you."

Beatrix peered around the post again, where the woman was looking right at her, a beaming smile across her lips.

"You… you can see me?" asked Beatrix.

"Yes, I can see you. And I can hear you too. I've always had a talent for these things. Is it okay if I come up there?"

Beatrix nodded, and the woman dashed across the hall, moving like an excited child, to the foot of the stairwell. She took the stairs two at a time and plonked herself on the step beside her.

"Hiya," she said. "I'm Lili. What's your name?"

"I… um… I'm Beatrix."

"Oh, I love that name! So old fashioned, you know? Just like mine, really. How long have you been here, Bea? Do you mind if I call you Bea? Or do you prefer Trixie?"

"Um… I don't…"

"Cool. I'll call you, Bea. You can call me Lili or Lil or whatever you want, really."

"Okay… um…"

"Christ, it's bloody freezing in here!" exclaimed Lili, pulling off her woolly hat and shaking out her black, bobbed hair.

"I don't feel the cold."

"Oh, of course. What with you being dead and all. Well, there have to be some benefits, don't there?"

"I suppose," grinned Beatrix. She liked this girl. Her usual anxiety of newcomers had melted away in moments under the frontal assault of Lili's loquacious affability.

"Always wanted to see this place," said Lili. "Heard it was gorgeous. You gonna show me around or what?"

"Um… yes, I suppose I can."

And so, Beatrix gave Lili the tour of Woodchester Mansion. She had memorised the various guides' patter, anecdotes, and history of the building over the years, though this was the first occasion where she had cause to deliver the script herself. She threw herself into it, adding increasing dramatic flair and subtle embellishments in each room. She was not sure why she felt the need to impress Lili. And when she caught the young woman's amused smile, Beatrix felt acutely self-conscious, and her voice faltered.

"Oh, don't stop," urged Lili. "I was enjoying that."

"You're making fun of me."

"No, I'm not, I promise. Listen… what about the Frenchman? The plasterer? Was it true he was murdered here? I heard he was bludgeoned to death after an argument."

"I can't say I've seen him around," shrugged Beatrix, stifling a giggle.

"Well, if you do see him, say 'bonjour' from me, will you?"

"I'll be sure to."

Beatrix led Lili upstairs to her favourite room, the one in which she spent most of her time. It offered the most beautiful view of the grounds and surrounding woodlands.

Lili took a seat at the window and stared out over the gardens, as the fine drizzle settled like a blanket over the wintery landscape.

"You never answered me," said Lili. "How long have you been here, Bea?"

Forlorn

"I… I don't know," Beatrix replied.

"Why are you here?" Lili pressed. "You didn't live here. From what I can gather, nobody did." Beatrix had no answer. She had often questioned this herself over the years, but the more she tried to focus on the events that led her to be at Woodchester, the more those thoughts slipped through her spectral fingers. It was like clinging to fog. All she could offer was a shrug.

"Then why do you stay?" asked Lili.

"Oh, I can't leave."

"Why? What's keeping you here? You could go anywhere."

"No, you don't understand, Lili," floundered Beatrix. "I *cannot* leave. Something stops me from passing the threshold. It's like… an invisible wall."

"Oh, that sucks."

"It's… fine," Beatrix assured her, though her tone lacked conviction. "I do so love this house. And I enjoy it when the visitors come, and I can spend time with them. Not that they've been here for some time."

Forlorn

"Of course," said Lili. "You can't continue like this forever though, Bea. You must get ever so lonely?"

Beatrix lowered her head and nodded slightly. She found it hard to put words to her feelings of isolation and seclusion. At times she wanted to curl into a ball and cry. At other times, she wanted to curse and scream and beat her fists against the wall at the sheer unfairness of it all.

"So, in all this time, am I the first person to actually see you?" asked Lili.

"Yes. Well... there was one other. But she ran away."

"That's terrible. You poor thing!"

"It's okay," shrugged Beatrix. "When people come here, I get to listen to their conversations, and I can pretend I'm participating. And I talk to the bats in the attic – they're very good company."

"With all due respect, that's bollocks, Bea," sneered Lili. "People are awful! Why do you give a shit about listening to their mundane nonsense?"

"Oh, they're not so bad."

"They *are* bad," snarled Lili. "People are terrible. They are the worst, Bea! You're just too nice to see it. If only you knew…"

"Knew what?" asked Beatrix.

Lili didn't answer. Her demeanour had changed entirely: her pleasant, playful manner was replaced with agitated annoyance, verging on barely contained fury, as she strode back and forth, clenching and unclenching her fists. She stopped and wheeled around to face Beatrix.

"What would you say if I told you I could help you leave this place?"

"What? How?"

"And what if I said I could teach you how to touch things? To pick them up? To hold them? To be seen and be heard whenever you want?"

"What do you mean, Lili?"

Lili strode across to Beatrix and dropped into a cross-legged sitting position on the floor before her.

"Come on – sit with me," she urged. Beatrix did as she was asked and knelt facing her new friend.

Forlorn

"Now, close your eyes," said Lili. "Concentrate on my voice. Relax and clear your mind."

Beatrix did as she was asked. Lili's soft voices washed over her, as the world began to fade away.

"I want you to focus, Bea," whispered Lili. "Think about the first time you came to Woodchester."

July, AD 1873

Beatrix Montague accepted the driver's hand and stepped down from the carriage, her shoes crunching on the drive's fresh gravel.

"Mister Leigh is here already, Ms Montague," he said. "He's expecting you."

"Thank you," said Beatrix. "Please wait for me. This won't take long."

Beatrix stood for a moment, taking in the fine mansion. It was certainly as impressive as her father had said – almost as grandiose as her own family home if a little ostentatiously modern for her tastes. She expected more noise from an active building site, though the place was deathly quiet today, with only the rush of the breeze through the trees and joyful sounds of birdsong disturbing the silence.

Beatrix took a deep breath, then strode towards the front door and raised her hand to rap on the freshly jointed, smooth planks, but the door was yanked open before her knuckles could make contact.

"Ah, you must be Ms Montague," said the stocky, well-dressed man on the other side. His cheeks and nose were flushed red, whilst the remaining strands of his strawberry-blonde hair were brushed across his balding pate.

"Mister William Leigh, I presume?"

"That's correct, my dear," he said, smiling broadly. "Please, do come in."

He stood aside, gesturing for her to enter. The smile never left his face, though Beatrix noted that it seemed restricted to his mouth, never straying to his eyes. A "huckster's grin", her father would have called it. He had warned her to be very careful of this man, believing him a gifted liar and grifter of the highest order. She stepped past him, noting the aroma of old port and cigars.

"Did you have a pleasant ride here?" Leigh asked. "Did my man Stanley look after you?"

"Yes, thank you, Mister Leigh. The scenery is beautiful – and Stanley is good company."

The interior of Woodchester Mansion was bare in comparison to the building's exterior – nothing but a bare shell, though the stonework was spectacular. Beatrix could easily see the potential in this property.

"What do you think?" asked the master of the house.

"It is certainly… impressive, Mister Leigh."

"Oh, please, call me Bill," he insisted. "Would you like some tea?"

"No, thank you, Mister Leigh," Beatrix insisted. "I am sure you realise my father has not sent me here on a social visit?"

"Very unusual for a young lady such as yourself to be working in a bank, Ms Montague. Never heard of such a thing before."

"My father's bank, Mister Leigh," Beatrix corrected. "He hopes that my sister and I will take over the bank's daily affairs, one day."

"How very progressive of him," the man patronised. He gestured to her left hand. "You're married woman, Ms Montague?"

"No," said Beatrix, clutching her right hand over the wedding band, protectively. "My late mother's ring, Mister Leigh. Just something to remember her by."

"I see," he smiled, with apparent sincerity. "I'm sorry for your loss, Ms Montague. Oh, where are my manners? Please, allow me to show you around."

"Please, Mister Leigh," pleaded Beatrix with increasing impatience. "I am here to discuss your account."

"Let's start upstairs," he continued, unabated. "You should see the progress we've made."

With that, William Leigh bounded away with exuberant enthusiasm, disappearing up the stairwell. Beatrix sighed and followed after. She found him in one of the first-floor bedrooms.

"This will be the main master bedroom," he declared. "As you can see, we've got the fireplace in already, with adjoining dressing room through there. And just look at this wonderful view. The window seats were my idea."

"Yes, yes, it's quite lovely, Mister Leigh," snapped Beatrix. "Might I ask why there are no workmen present today?"

"Oh, I've given them the day off."

"Is that so?" she said. "And not because you cannot afford to pay them?"

Leigh opened his mouth to protest, but then his shoulders slumped. He sighed deeply.

"How did you know?" he mumbled.

"I took a guess," said Beatrix. "You owe the bank a great deal of money, Mister Leigh. You have not made a repayment on your ten-thousand-pound loan in over six months. We also heard rumours that you were arrested for fighting with one of your workmen?"

"A mere misunderstanding, Ms Montague."

"Your arrest, or the default on your loan, Mister Leigh?"

For a moment, Beatrix thought the man might lunge at her. His eyes narrowed, his fists clenched, and his jaw flexed with fury. Leigh was clearly not used to having his word questioned, especially not by a woman.

"I am a man of my word, Ms Montague," he said, his words measured and controlled. "Please assure your father he will have his money."

"Of that, my father has no doubt, Mister Leigh. However, I am afraid he has lost patience with you. You have ignored every letter, every attempt to make contact. He is left with no option but to exercise provisions on the default terms of your loan."

"No!" gasped Leigh. "He cannot!"

"He can and he will, Mister Leigh," said Beatrix. "In fact, he already has."

She reached into her handbag and handed him a heavy, cream wove envelope.

"Court proceedings have already commenced, Mister Leigh. If you do not surrender the deed for this property forthwith, you will be found in contempt and incur further legal sanctions. You have twenty-four hours to comply and vacate the premises. Good day, Mister Leigh."

Beatrix turned and left the room, her mouth dry, heart-pounding, and blood rushing in her ears. She had been dreading this moment since her father revealed that he expected her to deliver the seizure and eviction notice personally. As she reached the top of the stairs, she felt no relief in having completed the task – she just wanted to get out of here and go home.

"You will not take my home!"

Beatrix spun around as Leigh stormed towards her, his face puce, the letter scrunched angrily in his fist. As she put down her foot, her heel slipped from the edge of the top stair. She teetered for a moment, waving her arms to keep her balance before the sickening lurch in the pit of her stomach as she succumbed to gravity. There was an excruciating crunch as the back of her head collided with the stone steps.

And then, nothing. Darkness.

There were flashes of memory. Just strands of recollection, but nothing that would stick. A night-time desert. A strange, robed man, his ebony skin covered in scars. Fear, confusion. Not afraid of this stranger, per se – she felt no malice from him. She was confused and scared. And so, Beatrix ran.

Forlorn

She found herself in Woodchester Mansion again, in the entrance hall, the daylight beginning to fade. What had happened? Where had the time gone? Her memory was an addled collision of random scraps of memory: of fear, and pain, and confusion.

Beatrix heard indistinct voices emanating from another room towards the building's rear. Two men, she guessed from the timbre of their speech. The tone of their exchange sounded agitated, though she could not make out the words.

"Hello?" she called out. There was no response, so she moved towards the speakers.

She discovered them in the drawing room – Mister Leigh and the carriage driver, Stanley. Even by the standards of the rest of the home's partial completion, this room was in disarray, with a section of wooden flooring at the room's centre torn up, with both men waist-deep in it, stripped to their vests, smeared with muck, shovelling dirt from the hole beneath. Nearby, a large bundle lay wrapped in a dustsheet.

"That should do it," said Leigh. "Come on."

The pair clambered from the hole and moved towards the bundle.

"Mister Leigh? What on earth is going on?" asked Beatrix. But the men ignored her.

Beatrix followed them over to the bundle, where Leigh knelt at one end.

"Please do not ignore me, Mister Leigh," snapped Beatrix, becoming increasingly irritated. A cold sensation washed over her and settled in the pit of her gut. She watched as Leigh twitched the dustsheet open to look upon what was concealed within the bundle. Beatrix moved behind the man and attempted to grip his shoulder, but her fingers passed right through him, creating a tingling sensation in her hand. Fear gripped Beatrix' heart, catching the air in her lungs. She stared at her slightly transparent hands in flustered bewilderment.

What was happening to her?

She looked down at the bundle, barely able to digest what lay before her. The object wrapped in the sheet was her. Eyes shut, expression peaceful, as though in restful slumber, though her dark hair was a sticky, matted mass and the sheet was stained red beneath her head.

"Come on, sir," said Stanley. "We're losing light. People will be asking questions."

Leigh nodded, glumly, his eyes glistening with tears. He covered her back over and the men took up a position at either end. They hoisted the body, staggered to the hole, and dumped it into the freshly dug pit.

"It was an accident, you know?" he told Stanley. "I didn't touch her. She fell."

"I know, sir," replied the impassive driver, as he took up his spade and began shovelling dirt back into the hole.

"It would ruin me, Stan."

"I know, sir."

"It's terrible, but why should it ruin my life too? I have responsibilities, Stan. People rely on me for their livelihood. People like you, Stan."

"I know, sir," said the carriage driver, pausing his shovelling for a moment. "I'll take this secret to my grave, sir."

"Just remember what we discussed," said Leigh. "You went to pick her up, as agreed, and she was not there. And so, you left."

"That's right, sir. Ms Montague never showed up."

"And you're sure nobody saw you?"

Forlorn

"I'm certain of it, sir," said Stanley. "I collected Ms Montague from her cottage on her father's grounds. She told me she does not keep a staff on the journey over here, sir. There was no-one else at the Montague House grounds, sir – not that I saw, at least."

"How could you?" whimpered Beatrix. "Please! You cannot just discard me like this. My father... my sister... they'll never know what happened to me. Please, you cannot do this! Please! I beg of you!"

It was no use – the men could not hear her. They continued to heap dirt into the hole. Covering her... her... body. Beatrix hated to think of it in that way. She turned and ran, overwhelmed with conflicted anger and misery. As she burst through the doorway, her shoulder collided with the drawing room door, barging the heavy timber aside. She fled for the entrance hall, desperate to get away from this place. To get home. Perhaps her sister would be able to see her? She had to try.

As Beatrix attempted to pass through the open front door, her hopes of escape were dashed. She rebounded from the opening and fell to the floor. She tried again, placing her hand against the portal, yet it was no use. She pushed against the invisible barrier, but it would not give. She battered against it, over and over, like a fly bouncing against a windowpane.

It was futile. She was trapped.

***

Beatrix looked down at the drawing room's dusty, unpolished wooden slats beneath her feet.

"I'm under there," she muttered, her tone morose, almost disbelieving. "How could they?"

"People!" spat Lili. "I'm never surprised at the depths to which they sink. They are evil!"

Beatrix turned to her companion, confused.

"You speak of them like you're not a person too, Lili."

Lili simply shrugged. "Looks can be deceiving, Bea. They would call me vile, malevolent, wicked, but I am *nothing* compared to them. They corrupt all they touch. They take, they steal, they kill, they *lie*! I will never lie to you, Bea."

"Who are you, Lili? *What* are you?"

Forlorn

"Your family believed you ran away, Bea, did you know that? Those men took your life, they buried you under the floorboard, trapping your spirit here, then they lied to those you loved – who loved *you*. They never had closure, Bea. They never knew the truth. Your father died believing his daughter hated him so much that she fled. He was consumed by guilt, Bea. He thought it his fault for forcing you to come here and deliver that letter. He never forgave himself. His bank did seize this property, you know? He never did anything with it, though. Couldn't bring himself to. He never realised his daughter was buried beneath the floorboards."

"How do you know this, Lili?" asked Beatrix. "How *could* you know it? Are you… are you like me? A spirit?"

"Not like you, Bea, no," said Lili. "Spirits were once human. People give my kind many names: demon, imp, fiend, devil. They fear us, though we never meant them harm. We were here first until they forced us from the world and into hiding. We are at one with nature – a part of the universe's natural order. We tried to maintain balance, but the humans did all they could to destroy and debase all things. And the more their numbers swelled, the more they consumed and the further into the darkness my kind retreated. No more, Bea! Now, we take a stand! We fight back. We will take this physical plane from them and emerge into the light once more. I'm building an army, Bea. We are legion and our numbers grow each day. You could join us?"

In the failing light, Lili's eyes appeared entirely black, although Beatrix could not be certain if that was a mere trick of her imagination.

"What do you mean, Lili?" she asked, backing away. "I... I don't want to hurt anyone. And what use would I be? I cannot even touch anything."

"You can if you choose," shrugged Lili, she picked up the hammer from where it stood propped against the fireplace. "It takes a force of will. Focus your strength – summon up your emotions and use them to apply force. Over time, you can learn to move physical objects. Even to seize them – to *use* them."

"Oh, great. So, I can give them a hand with the restorations then?" huffed Beatrix, rolling her eyes.

"Oh, you can do *so* much more than that, Bea," grinned Lili. "And when you figure that out, only then can you leave this place and join me. It takes a powerful, visceral act to break free, Bea. You must decide if you wish to join me – to fight back against the plague of humanity. Or you can stay here. Alone with your misery."

"What do you mean?" asked Beatrix. "What is it I must do?"

"When the time comes, you'll know what to do. I'll be seeing you very soon."

With that, Lili tossed the hammer towards Beatrix. She tried to catch it, but it slipped through her phantom fingers and clattered onto the floor. When she looked up, Lili was gone.

***

The days turned into weeks, then into months. Winter came and went, then turned into spring. The trees began to bud, wildflowers bloomed on the lawns and at the neighbouring wood's apron. Birds fluttered gleefully through the air, dropping to the lawn to pluck juicy worms from the ground, whilst squirrels gave chase through the trees, leaping from branch to branch in their endless game of tag.

Spring always lifted Beatrix's mood. She loved nature's rebirth – the fresh green of the grass, the leaves, the colourful petals of flowers, the blue of the sky, the fluttering of insects. But not this year. Since her encounter with Lili and the recollection of her death, Beatrix had become consumed. She dwelled on those final moments. How those men had hidden what they had done. They tossed her aside like a dead stray cat, with little regard.

And each day, her fury grew.

Every day, Beatrix followed Lili's advice – she focused her rage, her wretchedness, and applied it. After a couple of weeks, she found she could push a dried leaf across the entrance hall's floor. Just an inch or two, at first. With practice, she could pick up a leaf and cradle it in her palm. It would only remain there for a few seconds before falling to the floor again, but it was progress. With more practice, Beatrix was able to hold the leaf for as long as she could hold her concentration, before scrunching it in her fist.

Her strength grew. By the time the first blossoms flowered, Beatrix was able to raise both handles of the wheelbarrow in the study, half laden with broken bricks and push it several feet. And when she touched things, she could *feel* them. At times, she almost felt alive again.

*

Beatrix watched through the window as the approaching figure trudged up the drive. She recognised her at once, although this time she was not clad in dark clothes. Her puffy jacket was a bright, lurid yellow, whilst her hair was dyed cobalt blue rather than the green of the last time they met. It had grown somewhat since last winter too, and yet the girl was unmistakable. How could Beatrix ever forget the first person to see her in almost one-hundred-and-fifty years? She watched as the girl made her way towards the front door and disappeared through the opening into the entrance hall.

"Hello?" called out Meg. "Are you here?"

Beatrix waited for her in the drawing room. Listening intently to the clomp of the girl's combat boots on the wooden floor. That was another unexpected talent Beatrix had developed over the passing winter. She no longer needed to move from room to room like a human. She had learned she was no longer bound to the physical world, no longer truly a part of it, and she could manifest in any of Woodchester's many rooms in an instant, just by thinking of it.

"Oh, hello," said the girl as she entered the drawing room. She stopped by the doorway, radiating nervousness, almost hopping from one foot to the other.

"Hello," smiled Beatrix.

"I… I'm not sure if you remember me—"

"Of course I do. You're the girl who ran away when you saw me."

"Yeah, I'm sorry about that," blushed Meg. "It was a bit of a shock."

"Don't worry, I understand," assured Beatrix. "I would have done the same, no doubt, had the situation been reversed. Please, come in."

"Thank you," said the girl, taking tentative steps forward. "My name's Meg."

"It's nice to properly meet you, Meg. My name is Beatrix, but you can call me Bea. Can I ask why you have returned?"

Meg shifted, uncomfortably. "I've thought about you a lot since last time – couldn't stop thinking of you, to be honest. I felt… silly for running away. I mean, you just tried to say hello and I panicked."

"Please, think no more of it," smiled Beatrix.

"That's just it," said Meg. "I *can't* stop thinking about it. It's the most amazing thing I've ever witnessed. I mean, *you* are. And just lately, I keep dreaming of you. Every night. My dreams, telling me to come here. I saw how lonely you are, and I couldn't bear it. I mean, it's probably just my imagination, but I had to come and see you. I don't even know why I'm telling you this. It sounds silly, I know."

"Well, thank you, Meg," said Beatrix. "I thank you for coming. It can be awfully secluded here."

"I just thought you might need a friend. And I felt daft for being scared of you."

Beatrix nodded, smiling broadly.

"Again, thank you, Meg," she said. "Remind me why you and your friends were here."

"Oh... I... um... that's not important. We were just curious, really."

"Curious? Really? Is that so? So, you weren't here to take advantage of this abandoned building, regardless of what the consequences to others might be?"

"I'm not sure what you—"

"Why on earth would I want a drug-addicted brewer of poisons as a friend?" sneered Beatrix. "You and your criminal friends sell your foul wares to those who cannot help themselves. You destroy lives, without any consideration of what you do to them or to their families. Addicts steal and kill to make money to buy your toxic substances and you think nothing of their victims. You are a leech, Meg – a parasite. Those like you suck the life from the world and make it worse for all, a little at a time, day-by-day."

As Beatrix spoke, Meg began to back away.

"I... I don't know what you're talking about," protested Meg.

"Liar!" snapped Beatrix, advancing on the girl. "I can see inside your head, Meg. I know what you do. I know all about you. Your thoughts, your fears, even the things you won't admit to yourself. You're here even though your associates don't believe you about the Woodchester ghost because they need a new location for your lab. You're here to try and worm your way around me. To ask for my permission – the poor, lonely spirit, so desperate for company that I might ignore what you're doing, just for the privilege of being around you."

Eyes wide, Meg turned and dashed for the door, but Beatrix was already there, waiting for her.

"You were right to be scared, Meg," she whispered.

Forlorn

Beatrix did not even remember picking up the hammer, but there it was, clutched firmly in her right hand. She could feel the wood's grain against the ghostly flesh of her palm, its head reassuringly heavy. She swung it with all her might, connecting cleanly with the girl's temple with a nauseating crack. Meg crumpled to the floor, blood oozing from the fresh wound. Beatrix dropped the bloodied hammer then slumped to her knees, as though winded. Her head buzzed, full of static and noise, whilst every fibre of her being prickled with electricity, like cold water on a broken tooth. It built to a screaming crescendo which felt like it would never stop – pain without end. Like it was the only thing that existed. As though Beatrix and the agony of existence were one.

Until finally, breathlessly, it stopped.

Beatrix's vision cleared, her mind a swirling torrent of clearing fog. Her fingers trembled and every ghostly nerve twanged and tingled. She pushed herself up onto her knees and, using the wall for support, clambered to unsteady feet. Her head swam and she had to cling to the doorframe for a moment. She could touch. She could feel! Without having to concentrate either. The dust and dirt which coated the boards scraped and shifted beneath her boots as she moved. Her head throbbed, and a quick examination with probing fingers returned blood-smeared tips. She staggered back into the drawing room, heading for the fireplace mirror. But Beatrix already knew what she would see. She ran shaking fingers through her blue hair and traced her fingers over alien features, lingering on the piercings at her nose and eyebrow. Beatrix gulped, took a deep breath, exhaled through her plum-painted lips, and nodded in acceptance.

Beatrix hesitated at Woodchester Mansion's threshold. She had tried to pass this barrier countless times, only to be rebuffed on each occasion. She held her breath and raised a single foot, dangling it tentatively before lunging forward. It passed through the doorway with no resistance and landed on the porch step beyond. Beatrix stepped through and hurried to the gravel driveway, as though expecting to be dragged back inside at any moment.

She stood, blinking in the brittle spring sunshine, luxuriating in the weak rays and the cool breeze upon her face. She spread her arms wide, head thrown back, eyes screwed shut and laughed; a gentle giggle at first, developing into a full-throated cackle as tears streamed down her cheeks.

Forlorn

"I told you I'd be seeing you soon, Bea," said a nearby voice.

Beatrix opened her eyes, shielding them from the sun to focus on the newcomer just a few meters away, though she knew that voice without seeing its speaker. It was Lili. Beatrix grinned and rushed towards her, and the pair embraced like long-lost friends.

"You're free now, Bea," Lili cooed. She broke the embrace and put her arm around Beatrix' shoulders. The pair stared back at the old mansion.

"Now, let's get out of here," Lili said, a twinkle in her all-black eyes. "We've got a lot of work to do."

***

From the upstairs window, Meg watched the pair walk arm-in-arm along the driveway, heading away from the mansion. She banged her futile spectral fists against the glass, sobbing and screaming in dismay. Her silent cries echoed, unheard, around the halls of Woodchester. Her new forever home.

Of Older and Fouler Things

The Kingdom of the Dwarfs, beneath Cnámhdroma na Talún (the Spine of the World) mountain range, The Imperial Realm of Glaseód.

Mines are a dangerous place, as any pitman will gladly tell you. Therefore, they tend to breed a particularly stoic character, not given to flights of fancy or daydreams. This is particularly true of the dwarfs of Glaseód. They only trust what they can see and feel – and there is little more tangible than the risk that millions of tons of rock could come crashing down on your head at any moment due to an inattentively installed pit prop.

And yet, these stolid peoples still had their peculiar beliefs and traditions. One such superstition was in the existence of the denizens of deep mines, known as knockers. The dwarfs believed these knockers were gentle, playful spirits, possibly the ghosts of dearly departed colliery brothers and sisters. They thought the knockers kept them safe, protecting them from shaft collapses, gas explosions and more, by alerting them to impending doom. Many a fortunate miner owed his or her life to hearing a faint *tap, tap, tapping* on the beams, and got themselves to safety shortly before the world caved in.

And so, the miners left the mischievous imps scraps of food to appease them: half-eaten sandwiches, pieces of fruit, scraps of cake, anything that miners kept in their lunch pails.

However, the knockers were not the only things in the darkness. That's why the miners needed all the help they could get.

King Erik scratched at his thick, greying beard and accepted the iron helmet offered to him by his personal assistant, Simeon.

"This shouldn't take too long, sir," said Simeon. "It's a quick meet and greet. The shaft foreman will show you their latest discovery, you act suitably impressed, give a wave to the subjects, perhaps pose for a quick etching, and then we're out of here."

Erik huffed and gave a reluctant nod of understanding, his expression grim. He hated these bloody junkets. Oh, Simeon did his best and he was good at his job, for sure, but all too often Erik felt like some sort of performing animal, wheeled out for his subjects to point and cheer. He was supposed to be king, for the gods' sake! Should it not be the other way around? Were his subjects not supposed to do what *he* said?

"Are you ready, sir?" asked Simeon.

Erik was not entirely sure he trusted his chief advisor. He was so… un-dwarf-like. Simeon had gone to school in the big city at Murias where he had learnt to comport himself with poise and refinement – to speak with kings and commoners alike. He was slightly taller and certainly more slender than most dwarfs, and lacked the proper beard, having styled his facial hair to be trim, short, and neat, with a thin moustache merging with the whiskers of his chin, whilst his cheeks were clean-shaven up to his short sideburns. He did not talk like a dwarf either. Simeon insisted that his education taught him the value of good diction, which he had assured Erik was not as filthy as it sounded.

However, duty called. King Erik fastened his iron safety helmet's strap and rapped it with his knuckles.

"Right, let's get this over with," he sighed.

Of Older and Fouler Things

"Welcome to Shaft #14, Yer 'Ighness," greeted shaft foreman Fred. "The lads are reet excited to see you down 'ere."

"And lasses," nudged shift leader Doris, jogging her boss's elbow.

"And lasses," grinned Fred, without breaking stride. "We've got a reet good mix dahn 'ere, an' no mistake."

"Good, good," said King Erik, approvingly. "Me old mam were the best bloody dredger I ever worked with – could chisel wi' the best o' 'em. Worked 'er knuckles to the bone, she did. Discovered some o' the best minerals we've seen in these parts in an age."

"Aye, well let me tell you, we've made some great finds in Shaft #14 these past few months, Yer 'Ighness," said Fred. "In't that right, Doris?"

"Aye," chimed in Doris. "Solid core of iron ore and some speckling of copper and gold, too."

"Aye, that's right," confirmed Fred. "But this… this is a bit special."

The foreman led the king and his entourage of guards, aides, and various royal hangers-on deeper into the shaft, whilst King Erik graciously returned the deferential glances and nervous smiles of the various miners they passed with a brief nod. Those that had any experience of King Erik knew what a big deal that was. It was as expressive as the dwarf king ever got. It was his equivalent of a hug.

Several hundred meters deeper into the shaft and they arrived at the main attraction.

"An' 'ere we are, Yer 'Ighness," proclaimed a triumphant Fred.

"Oh, my…" mumbled King Erik, for once lost for words.

"That's right," said Fred. "It were Doris's shift what uncovered it. A shelf o' solid marble – at least thirty feet long and four feet thick. And we don't know how deep it goes yet, but we think it's pretty hefty from our exploratory drilling."

"Bloody hell, lass, that's a crackin' find," King Erik said, addressing Doris directly. "You deserve a reward for this. Name it an' it's yours, girl."

"Oh, that's not necessary, Yer 'Ighness," blushed Doris.

"No, no," said the king. "I'm a man of conviction, Doris, an' I believe thems that do good work should be properly rewarded. So, what can I do for yer?"

Of Older and Fouler Things

"Um, well... if you insist, Yer 'Ighness," said Doris. "Perhaps a share in the profits from this seam?"

"Woah, woah, let's not be too hasty, Doris," backtracked Erik. "I were thinkin' a day off. Paid, like. Perhaps a cake."

"Ne'er mind 'er, Yer 'Ighness," interrupted Fred. "Doris is just doin' 'er job, in't that right, Doris?"

"Um... I s'pose—"

"And she dun't need no special treatment. In't that ri... sir?"

Fred had lost his king's attention, though, as the supreme ruler of the dwarf kingdom's eye had been drawn to a group of nearby miners. He wandered off, heading toward the group of dwarfs who were hunkered around a couple of wooden benches eating lunch.

"Afternoon, lads," he greeted. "No, dun't stand up on my account." He took a seat on one of the small wooden benches and accepted the wordlessly offered half-sandwich from the dwarf opposite.

"Oooo, cheese and pickle," said King Erik, approvingly. "Very nice. My compliments to your lady wife."

Of Older and Fouler Things

"Yer welcome, Yer 'Ighness," nodded the dwarf, respectfully. "Our Anne will be thrilled ter 'ave the king hisself eatin' one of 'er butties[2], sir."

"What are your name's lads?" asked Erik, stuffing the last of the sandwich into his mouth.

"I'm Charlie," said the sandwich benefactor. "And this 'ere is Alf, Reg, an' Colin."

"Good to meet you, lads," said Erik, oozing sincerity. And it was true. At heart, Erik still saw himself as a working dwarf. He missed his days "dahn't pit", getting a proper sweat on – working with tools down in the dirt. But now, it simply would not do for a king to be seen performing manual labour, or so his royal advisors had informed him.

"I couldn't help noticin' what you were doin' wit' yer butties," he continued. "What's that all about?"

The dwarfs exchanged embarrassed glances. Erik had watched each of the dwarfs tear a section from one of their sandwiches and leave the scrap on the ground. He had seen this many times back in his younger days of working in the mines, but his father, the old king, steadfastly refused to answer his

---

[2] Butties = slang for sandwiches.

questions on the subject. Erik had not thought about this odd practice in an age.

"Um… we're not s'posed to talk about it, Yer 'Ighness," mumbled Charlie, avoiding eye contact with his king.

"Well now," said Erik, his voice dripping with honeyed sweetness. "I mean, I'm not one for airs and graces and all that stuff, but I'm fairly certain that one o' us 'ere is king in these parts. Is it you Charlie?"

"No, sir," grumbled Charlie.

"No? Oh, then it must be *you*, Colin? No? Reggie? Alf?"

Each of the dwarfs shook their heads, eyes locked to the ground.

"Oh, silly me," said Erik. "Then who is king, Charlie?"

"Um… you're king, Yer 'Ighness," muttered Charlie.

"That's bloody right, lad," snarled Erik. "An' I'm pretty bloody sure that when yer king asks you a question, you'd better bloody-well gi' him an answer!"

Erik's raised voice echoed around the shaft as all eyes turned toward him and the group of besieged miners.

"Now, let me ask again," he said, sweetly. "What the deal with the butties?"

"Um... they're for the knockers, Yer 'Ighness," said Charlie.

"Knockers?"

"Um, perhaps we should move on, Your Highness?" suggested Simeon, obsequiously, appearing at his king's side without having seemingly moving his feet. One of his more unnerving talents.

"Gods, lad! We should put a bell on you!" exclaimed Erik. "An' there's no rush. I'm just sharing a sarnie an' a yarn wi' me new mates here."

"But sir—"

However, Simeon's protest ceased abruptly when he caught the king's furious glare. Chief amongst the advisor's talents was a knack for self-preservation, though he was certain to hear about this infraction later. At length. And volume.

"Anyway, lads," continued Erik. "You were tellin' me about these... what you call 'em? Knockers?"

"Aye, sir," continued Alf. "Mine spirits, sir. We leaves 'em food an' they warns us o' mine dangers. They looks out fer us, sir."

"Oh gods…" muttered Simeon. "Here we go."

"Woah, 'ang on," said King Erik. "You mean to tell me, you lot 'ave been wastin' perfectly good food all these years to leave tributes to bloody ghosts?"

"Not ghosts, Yer 'Ighness," protested Charlie. "Mine spirits. I mean, some believes they're the souls o' ol' miners who lost their lives in the dark, 'ere to warn us o' disasters an' suchlike. Others believes they've alus bin 'ere. They looks after us, so's we looks after them."

"Sounds like bloody daft superstition to me," sneered Erik.

With that, Charlie rolled up the cuff of the heavy fabric trousers, revealing his lower left leg. Well… what had once been his leg. Where the limb had once been was a shiny, metallic appendage running from his knee and disappearing into his brown leather hobnailed boot.

"Mine collapse, five year ago, sir," he explained. "Shaft #19, remember it?"

Of Older and Fouler Things

"Aye, I do at that, lad," confirmed Erik. He remembered it well. They had lost six good dwarf's that day when the diggers tapped into a patch of chalk, previously undiscovered by the survey team. The whole shaft came down on top of the shift crew. It was a miracle only six were killed.

"Jus' moments afore the collapse, I 'eard it, sir," continued Charlie. "I were tekkin' a quick water break an' there it was. *Tap, tap, tap... Tap, tap, tap...* Ne'er heard it afore, nor since, sir. I din't know what to think. It kept going. *Tap, tap, tap... Tap, tap, tap.* An' then I realised: It were a warnin', sir. I called out to the lads[3], an' we dropped tools an' 'eaded for t' shaft top. But it were too late, sir. Most got out safe, but me an' 'alf a dozen others got caught when't roof came down. I were pinned... leg trapped, rubble on top o' me. Thought I were a goner, sir. Ne'er felt pain like it. I could feel the stone, crushing't life out o' me. I were dead, for sure. I blacked out, but when I came to, someone had dragged me out o' the rubble an' left me where I were found by t' rescue team. They 'ad to tek me leg, but I were the lucky one. Six o' me brothers and sisters were not so fortunate."

---

[3] General term used by dwarfs for a group of mining colleagues, regardless of gender or status.

Of Older and Fouler Things

In the solemn silence that followed, King Erik sighed, nodding in earnest consideration of Charlie's tragic tale.

"Nah, I'm not 'avin' that," Erik said, eventually. "I dun't hold wi' that supernatural bollocks. Listen, lads: the mines are a treacherous mistress. Oh, they treat yer well most o' t' time. They gi' yer precious metals an' jewels an' stone, an' they mekes us all feel like kings. But she can turn, ha' no doubt, like the vicious bitch she is, an' rain down catastrophe on yer 'ead wi' no warnin'. It 'as nowt to do wi' ghost, or ghoulies, or elves, or pixies—"

"Actually, sir," interjected Simeon, "we know elves and pixies are real."

"Shut up!" growled Erik, without pausing. "All's I'm sayin' is the mine is no place fer fantasies an' tall tales. I believe in *real* things – things I can *touch*! I believe in stone, an' iron, an' dirt, an' sweat, an' gold... 'specially gold. There's no room dahn 'ere in t' dark fer daydreaming an' superstition. That crap will get yer killed. An' no more o' this wastin' food bullshit neither! It attracts rats, for one thing. I want an end ter this nonsense, yer 'ear me?"

The assembled group of miners looked at the floor, shamefaced, in mumbled acceptance.

"Excellent!" declared Simeon, clapping his hands, and rubbing them together in industrious fashion. "Now that's settled, we really should be getting on, sir. Lots to do, and all that. Gentlemen, it was a delight to meet you, but I'm sure you appreciate that King Erik is a very busy dwar—"

"Woah, woah," interrupted Erik, rising to his feet and cocking his head to one side. "What's that?"

"What's what, Your High—?"

"Shhhhhh!"

Erik caught it again, even above the general hubbub and background thuds of pickaxe and hammer, a sharp, rhythmic rapping, cutting across all other sounds.

Tap, tap, tap. Tap, tap, tap.

Eyes widened, he turned and caught Charlie's terrified stare.

"Everybody out!" Erik roared.

Without a word, all assembled dwarfs dropped whatever they were carrying and sprinted for the shaft entrance as a low rumbling, gathering in intensity, drowned out the tapping.

And then the world went dark.

Of Older and Fouler Things

***

Erik came to, his head thudding, and the air filled with choking dust. His eyes cast about in the pitch black, whilst his mind performed the standard reboot stocktake: are all four limbs in working order? Any suspicious pains or oozing? Is my beard okay?

He rolled onto his back and felt around. His fingers traced rocks and clods of mud to his left and above his head, with a clear space before his face. He reached as far as he could stretch, sitting up until his fingers felt the smooth surface above. A good few feet of head-clearance, if he was any judge. A sizeable air pocket, which was good. The bigger the pocket, the longer they could survive. Because, when the air ran out… Erik shook that thought loose. He did not want to think about that eventuality just yet.

"Anyone else in 'ere?" he whispered. Keeping the noise down was essential. Whilst he might be safe for now, Erik had no idea how precariously balanced the pile of rubble above him might be. Even the slightest tremor or disturbance could shake it loose and bring it crashing down.

"I'm here, Your Highness," hacked Simeon.

There were a chorus of groans and coughs which signalled a handful of others were similarly trapped in this small space.

"Hang on," hissed another. A spark flashed, blinding Erik momentarily. Once, twice, three times, before it settled into a steady glow as the oil lamp's wick caught. It was the shift leader, Doris, the one who had discovered the seam of marble.

"You okay, Yer 'Ighness?" she whispered, crawling over to him.

"Yeah, I'm fine," he said, removing his helmet and inspecting the deep dent in its outer shell, then fingering the corresponding welt on his bloodied temple. This thing had surely saved his life.

He surveyed the air pocket and the motley crew of five survivors. Only he, Simeon, Doris, Alf, and Colin had been lucky enough to be caught in this space, which was a few feet high and a couple of meters across. Above their heads, the shelf of marble had come to their rescue, propped up by piles of granite, and holding back the groaning rubble from snuffing out this tiny compartment. He could only hope the others had been as lucky.

"Anyone see what became o' t'others?" he asked, though their dark looks told him all he needed to know.

"Fred's gone," said Doris, her voice hoarse, eyes staring into the middle distance. "He shoved me forward as the roof came down. A 'orse-sized block o' granite crushed him afore the lights went out. He saved my life."

"I'm so sorry for your loss, Doris," comforted Simeon.

"Nah, I 'ated the bastard," shrugged Doris. "Worst boss I ever bloody 'ad. He were thick as an 'ousbrick sandwich, but he still din't deserve that."

"What about Charlie?" asked Erik, though Alf just shook his head and wiped a surreptitious tear from one eye.

"So, what do we do now, Your Highness?" asked Simeon.

"We wait," sighed Erik. He shrugged off his jacket, rolled it up and used it to make a pillow. Then he lay back, linking his fingers behind his head, and closed his eyes.

"What? We j-just wait?" stammered an ashen-faced Simeon. "What are we waiting for?"

"If we're lucky, someone'll come lookin' fer us. If we're *really* lucky, they'll gets 'ere afore air runs out."

"What? Is… is that a thing? W-we can't j-just wait whilst we slowly suffocate. Can't we… I don't know, can't we dig our way out?"

"Calm down, lad," said Erik. "There's nowt to be done. We move one wrong stone an' the 'ole bloody lot'll collapse in on us. Trust me – best thing to do reet now is wait. Save yer breath, lad – the air'll last longer."

With that, Simeon clamped his mouth shut and slumped into sullen silence. Erik took a deep breath, closed his eyes, and snoozed.

Both Erik's first and second wives often commented that the dwarf king could sleep through an earthquake. He had done just that, in fact. More than once. It was a knack most dwarf miners shared with soldiers – an ability to sleep in the blink of an eye, no matter how uncomfortable, dangerous, or noisy their surroundings. And Erik had been both a miner and a soldier in his past – he had developed this ability into a fine art.

Of Older and Fouler Things

"Wake up, Your Highness!" urged Simeon, and Erik's eyes sprung open. Another skill of the king was the capacity to rise to full, alert wakefulness as quickly as he had slipped into unconsciousness.

"What is it, lad?" he asked.

"Listen," whispered the advisor.

Erik heard it right away – a low, steady scratching and scraping, growing louder with every passing second.

"Is the roof going to collapse?"

The king silenced Simeon by putting a finger to his lips, then pressed his ear against the nearby wall.

"Diggin'?" he mused.

"What? That's amazing!" gasped Simeon. "We're saved!"

"Not so fast, lad," frowned King Erik. "It's not coming from t' shaft entrance. There's nowt this side o' us fer two 'undred yards. It mekes no sense. Whatever's diggin' through, it in't one o' our lot."

The scratching and scraping grew louder, and clods of dirt began to crumble and break away from the wall.

Of Older and Fouler Things

"Move back," urged Erik, scrambling away from the wall. He picked up a discarded pickaxe and clasped it in both hands, holding it before him as though warding off a vampire.

As the noise increased, the wall crumbled with greater intensity until, suddenly a large chunk broke away and crashed into the space in a shower of dust, leaving a gaping hole directly ahead. And from it, emerged a pair of massive, brown-haired hands, with long, gnarled fingers, each tipped with yellowing, chipped nails. The hands gripped the sides of the hole and their owner hauled itself through the gap and heavily plonked into the cavity, before shaking itself off like a wet dog.

"What on earth…?" gasped Erik.

It was the strangest creature the king had ever seen in all his years in Cnámhdroma na Talún's subterranean depths. It was short – no more than two feet tall, though its spindly arms extended fully to the ground, where its huge man-like hands could splay flat against the surface. It had a pear-shaped body with a potbelly, whilst its legs, such as they were, were squat haunches, with oversized, shovel-like feet and thick, clawed toenails. Its head was a squished oval, with large eyes and ears, a button nose, and a broad mouth. It was covered from head to toe in dirt-brown, suede-like fur. Undeterred by Erik's pickaxe, it ambled forward, propelling itself by placing its hands on the ground, hoisting its rump into the air, and thrusting its feet forward. It looked surprisingly nimble.

"Hello," it croaked. "Are you all okay?"

"What the devil are you?" gasped Erik, the axe trembling in his hands.

"Can't you tell, sir?" grinned Alf. "It's a knocker."

"What is a knocker?" asked the creature.

"Um... *you* are," answered Alf.

"Oh, really?" frowned the knocker, scratching his tiny chin with one lengthy digit. "Everyone just calls me Nohm. Those like me, we call ourselves the mouldywarp... Like you, we live under the ground. This place is our home."

"It's not your home," growled Erik, "it's a mine."

"It's your home too?" replied Nohm.

"No, well yes. But I mean it's a mine. It's all mines."

"Then you're very lucky to call this all a-yours," said Nohm, approvingly. "And I thank you for sharing it with us."

Erik opened his mouth to reply but stopped himself.

Of Older and Fouler Things

"Are you the one who warned us about the mine collapse?" asked Simeon.

"Yes," replied Nohm, nodding enthusiastically. "That's what my kind do. If we sense disturbances or shifts in the strata, we try to alert the bigguns—"

"Bigguns?" asked Simeon.

"Yes, you people," continued Nohm. "The other diggers, like us. We try to alert you before any disastrous events. Today, there was no time. It happened too fast."

"Well, thanks, lad," said Erik, begrudgingly. "Us five might not 'a' made it were it not fer you."

"What caused the collapse?" asked Doris. "I bin doin' the survey on this shaft an' there were nothin' t' suggest this might 'appen. No warnin' signs – nothin'."

"No time to talk now," insisted Nohm. "This space is not safe – it could collapse at any moment. Come with me and I will explain all."

With that, the knocker turned and disappeared into the hole from whence he came. Erik and the others watched him go.

"Come on," came Nohm's muffled voice, echoing from the tunnel.

Erik huffed but led the way. He crawled into the hole, which was just wide enough to accommodate his burly frame and followed Nohm into the darkness.

***

"Stop bloody pushin'!"

"It's not me, Your Highness," replied Simeon's muffled voice. "*They're* pushing *me*."

"Just get yer face out me backside!"

At that moment, with significant momentum from behind, Erik pitched forward and crashed into the space beyond, landing in a clattering heap with each of the other four landing on top of him, one after the other.

"Gerrof!" he exclaimed, struggling to extricate himself from the groaning pile of dwarf limbs. Erik pulled himself to his feet and looked around the small cavern, illuminated by the dim light of Doris's lamp. It was twice as large as the air pocket from which they had just escaped and its ceiling was high enough to stand. Dozens more tunnels, identical to the one from which they had just emerged, branched off from the hollow in every direction. The floor was littered with objects: old, dented lunch pails, broken oil lamps, pickaxe handles, broken shovels, cracked helmets. Nothing useful – simply the discarded detritus of the mine. And at its heart stood Nohm, grinning proudly.

"What is this place?" gasped Simeon.

"An' what's wi' all the tat?"

"This is my burrow," said Nohm, spreading his lanky arms wide. "And *this* is my collection."

"'Ow many bloody 'oles a' you dug, dahn 'ere, lad?" demanded King Erik. "Are you causin' my cave-ins?"

"No!" insisted Nohm. "My people are cautious about where we dig our burrows and tunnels, careful not to undermine the strata. We only dig where it will not harm your special tunnels. We only wish to co-exist with you."

"How do you survive down here, Nohm?" asked Simeon.

"Oh, we live off grubs, and insects, and worms, and mice, and rats – we especially like rats. In the spring, we tunnel nearer the surface, where we can catch rabbits. And, of course, we are always grateful for the scraps you leave for us."

"Ah, so you do eat those too?" grinned Alf.

"Oh, no," grimaced Nohm. "We *collect* them. They add some colour to our burrow... after a while at least. And the spores that form provide useful medicine when we are sick... well, sometimes..."

"Well, that explains the stink dahn 'ere," muttered Erik, kicking away what he dearly hoped was a half-eaten sausage near his boot.

"We like your people," continued Nohm. "You dig, like us, which can be dangerous. And so, when we sense a disturbance – a shift in the seams or lodes – we try to alert you."

"You mentioned others like you, Nohm," said Simeon. "Where are they?"

"I fear I am alone, now," sighed the knocker, his face a picture of misery, oversized eyes glistening. "I cannot find any of my people. There used to be many of us. However, there are other things here... in the darkness... They dig too, and they care little for the danger they pose."

"I ne'er 'eard o' nothin' like that dahn, 'ere," sneered Erik.

"With respect," replied Nohm, "You had never heard of us before today. Besides, they are new – they only arrived in recent days. They are terrifying! They dug into our burrows, took my wife... my children. I only escaped their clutches by the skin of my claws."

"What are they?" shuddered Simeon.

"I do not know. They are vicious monsters – all eyes, and legs, and teeth."

A low rumble echoed around the burrow and dirt and stones showered down on them from the ceiling.

"We must go," said Nohm. "It is not safe here. Those things have undermined this entire stratum. And they are attracted by noise. They will come for us. I will lead you to safety."

"Right," said Erik, a practical dwarf at heart. He did not need to know any more about these creatures – that could wait. "Which way is out?"

"Most of my tunnels have collapsed, or are occupied by those… beasts," said Nohm. "There is only one way out and it is hazardous."

The knocker raised his eyes to the ceiling.

"Up?" said Erik. The king was intimately acquainted with the topology of his mines and he had the wonderful sense of direction common to all subterranean dwellers. "There's only Shaft #6 up there. That's good – I've got a team o' lads working there right now."

"Not so good, I fear," quavered the knocker. "Your tunnels above are where the creatures have taken residence. That is where they took my tribe. They're all gone. We must pass through the monsters' lair to escape."

***

"I dun't buy it," whispered Erik. "My lads en't said nothin' 'bout no beasts in 'ere."

"And yet, where are they, Your Highness?" reasoned Simeon.

Of Older and Fouler Things

And Erik had to reluctantly concede that his advisor was right. A mineshaft was usually a hive of activity – the pounding of axe on stone, of shovel on dirt, of hand-drills, stone-crushers, the clanking of carts, and even the chunter of conversation and laughter. Yet here in Shaft #6 today, there was dead silence.

"There should be twenny o' 'em dahn 'ere," grunted the king. "I sen' 'em in meself. If owt's 'appened to 'em…"

As a veil of gloom draped over him, Nohm reached out one massive paw and placed it on Erik's shoulder.

"I hope your people are safe," said the knocker. "But I fear the worst. These creatures are fearsome and numerous. We must get ourselves to safety then determine what to do about them later."

"Aye, you're right," conceded Erik. "Come on – shaft entrance is this way."

Erik led them through the dark tunnels, holding Doris's lamp aloft, its wick turned to its lowest ebb to conserve oil and draw less attraction from prying eyes. They paused at each turn and Erik peered around the corner for any unwanted visitors. They crept, ears cocked, alert… listening for any alien sound. As Erik's traced the shaft's wall with probing fingers, he encountered something sticky, unpleasant, bonding his fingers together. He tore them away from the surface and examined the mucilaginous substance in the light.

"Oh, bugger," he groaned.

"What is it, Your Highness?" hissed Simeon.

"I think I know what we're dealing wi' 'ere. I think we got an infestation o' bloody básscáth."

"Are you sure?"

"Yeah, pretty sure," he sighed. "The one standin' just there is a big clue."

Simeon spun around to look down the tunnel. Staring at them, just ten feet away, was the largest, most terrifying spider the royal advisor had ever seen. Glistening black, with spiny hairs protruding from its thorax, abdomen and its eight spindly legs. It was the size of a large goat, its mandibles dripping with foul saliva. As they watched, the beast was joined by three others, merging from the darkness of the tunnel's walls and ceiling, before dropping heavily to the floor.

"Run!" screamed Erik.

***

Of Older and Fouler Things

Erik had never seen a básscáth before, yet they haunted his nightmares as a child when his nanny told him stories of these monsters. The giant, spider-like beasts were rumoured to be indigenous to the forbidden frozen wastes of Fomoria in the far north, with a venom that could paralyse a horse in seconds. Like spiders, they would then wrap their stricken prey in a cocoon of silk, feasting on their liquified innards later. Though as he grew older, Erik came to believe of these chilling brutes as nought but tales, designed to inspire fear in a child's impressionable mind. These days, he was far more fearful of more mature terrors – such as income tax.

However, world-weary cynicism tends to melt away under the blast-furnace heat of dreadful certainty. So now, he ran, with the terrible thud, thud, thud of their pursuers' legs echoing around them. He dared not look back to see how many were in pursuit.

He heard a cry from behind as the creatures caught up with one of their number, though their screams quickly muffled and faded as the chase continued.

Just then, another dog-sized básscáth dropped into view ahead, blocking their escape. Without slowing his stride, Erik snatched up a fallen hand-shovel from the ground and thrust it between the creature's many eyes. It smashed through the beast's skull with a satisfying crunch, and it collapsed, dead.

There, ahead, was another lamp, pitched on its side, its flame burning bright where its owner must have recently dropped it. He grabbed it, turned, and hurled it with all his might at the pursuing básscáth. It struck the ground immediately before the leading creature and shattered, showering it with burning oil. The flames spread quickly, engulfing the chasing pack. One made it through the pile, its body ablaze, as Erik brought the shovel down on its screaming head, finishing it off.

He looked around their diminished group – only he, Nohm, Simeon and Doris had survived the chase. Alf and Colin had not made it. He nodded, releasing a sorrowful sigh and said a silent prayer for his fallen compatriots.

Safe digging, my friends. May your seams be fruitful and your ores plentiful.

"Come on, we can't stay 'ere," he said. "There'll be more where them bastards came from."

And a hundred yards further on, Erik's heart sank further. Oh, how he hated being right sometimes.

Of Older and Fouler Things

The tunnel opened out into a huge cavern, at least thirty feet across and more than twice that high. Suspended far above their heads was the largest web Erik had ever seen. It stretched across the expanse, with dozens of chrysalides – some dwarf-sized, others smaller – tangled in its spirals and whorls. And there, at its hub sat the mother of all básscáth – their queen. She was as large as a cow, and right now, all eight of her eyes hungrily ogled the dwarven intruders. The walls of the hollow were bedecked with thousands of her children, like the most chilling wallpaper imaginable.

"We didn't dig this, did we?" Simeon gasped. Erik slowly shook his head, hardly able to comprehend what lay before his eyes.

"I think we know what's caused the cave-in," said the king. "These the same buggers what snatched your family, Nohm?"

"Yes," trembled the knocker, cowering behind Erik.

"Who goes there?" boomed the queen, with a voice like the scratching of nails on coffin lids. "Who dares stray into my eyrie?"

Of Older and Fouler Things

Erik summoned up all his royal hauteur and gravitas. "I am Erik t' fifteenth, King o' Cnámhdroma na Talún, Chief Excavation Controller, Commander o' t' Dwarf Legion, an' Supreme Overlord o' t' Dwarf Nation – an' *you* are in *my* domain, girl! Uninvited, I might add."

However, the dwarf king's grandiose statement did not have the desired effect. After a moment's silence, a booming cackle echoed around the chamber, like the wheezing smoker's cough of some great giant. The queen was laughing at him. At *him*! Her laughter was accompanied by the dutiful chittering of her many, many children.

"*Royalty?*" hooted the queen. "*I am honoured by your presence, my liege. I would curtsy if I could.*"

Erik was grateful for the low light so that the others could not see his cheeks burning crimson, or the spark of fear in his eyes as the giant spider began her descent from the web to the cavern floor, lowering herself by a single strand of silk.

"*I have never eaten a monarch before,*" continued the básscáth queen. "*I wonder if blue blood tastes better?*"

"Leave this to me, Your Highness," said Simeon, stepping between the giant spider and his ruler.

"What yer doin' lad?" hissed Erik.

"My job is to act as your envoy, sir – to converse with kings and queens on your behalf. When the tyrant Rí Mhórdúil came here, demanding your fealty, did I not successfully negotiate our nation's independence in return that we supply his armies with superior, dwarf-made weapons?"

Erik shuddered at the memory of Rí Mhórdúil. Simeon was right – that brute was certainly more terrifying even than this creature.

"O' course, lad," admitted the king. "Credit where it's due, yer did a good job. Just be careful, eh?"

"Thank you, sir," said the advisor. He turned back to the básscáth queen, put on his most obsequious smile, and stepped forward.

"Your Majesty," he said, offering her a sycophantic bow, "I am Simeon, Chief Advisor to King Erik the Fifteenth, King of Cnámhdroma na Talún, Chief Excavation Controller, Commander of the Dwarf Legion, and Supreme Overlord of the Dwarf Nation. And you are?"

"Hungry!" growled the básscáth queen. She lurched forward with the speed of a python, clamping her mandibles around Simeon's skull. Her jaws snapped shut, snipping off the dwarf's head without any apparent effort.

"Bloody run!" roared Erik. The remaining trio dashed for the opening on the cavern's other side.

"After them!" commanded the queen, though her voice was partially muffled as she masticated the royal advisor's cranium. Her children poured down the walls like water, flooding into the tunnel in hot pursuit of the dwarf king.

"This way," whispered Erik.

They had given the básscáth the slip several minutes earlier in the network of tunnels. Erik knew these passages intimately – better than even his most experienced pitmen – and was able to navigate every turn and linkway without losing his bearings.

When the básscáth moved as a group, their footfall gave away their positions, enabling the dwarfs and the knocker to remain out of their clutches. The entrance was close now – once they emerged from the final side-tunnel, it was a hundred-yard dash to the heavy gate that barred their exit. And they would still need to open it, get out, and slam it shut before the beasts could get them. Their chances were slim, but the king was not prepared to roll over and die just yet. Doris, however, was disconsolate. Tears rolled down her cheeks and she sobbed uncontrollably the closer they came to the exit. She too had clearly worked out the challenge that faced them in this final leg.

"Listen t' me, lass," said Erik, "Dun't you go givin' up on me now, eh? We need to stay together, reet? We're gonna make it, yer 'ear me?"

She nodded, wiping her eyes, her bottom lip quivering.

"Good girl," he said, before turning to Nohm. "You ready, lad?"

"I'm ready," replied the knocker.

Suddenly, a loud, grating, metallic noise echoed from the main tunnel. Erik poked his head around the corner and, sure enough, the shaft's entry gate was groaning open. His heart skipped with glee as, on its other side, a horde of heavily armoured dwarf troopers spilled into the tunnel. But then, a thunderous roar, like the pounding of thousands of hooves, erupted from the tunnel's other end as básscáth of every shape and size surged forward – on the walls, floor, even the ceiling, clambering over each other in their urge to reach the exit. If the creatures made it out of this shaft, not only was the mine lost, but the entire kingdom would fall. They were doomed!

"Now!" cried Erik. "Go! Go! Go!"

The three emerged from their hiding place and headed for the gate, sprinting as fast as their legs would carry them with stampeding death not far behind. The squad of dwarves poured past their king to engage the enemy with battle-axe, sword, and mace. They slowed the básscáth throng, though they could not hold them indefinitely and would soon be overwhelmed. Even in the thick of battle, they could not prevent a few básscáth slipping past them to continue their pursuit.

As they neared safety, Doris fell behind and, with just thirty yards to go, disaster struck – she stumbled and fell, and one of the creatures was on her in a heartbeat. She disappeared in a tangle of teeth and legs. The other básscáth pair continued after Erik and Nohm. Suddenly, the knocker stopped in his tracks.

"What yer doin'?" screamed Erik. "Are yer daft, lad?"

"Go," said Nohm, his voice level and calm, yet determined. The look in the knocker's eyes brooked no argument. They shared a nod of respect, from one miner to another, then Erik turned and fled. As he reached the gate he turned and hauled the heavy timbers on their greased runners across the shaft's doorway, just in time to see the little knocker bring down the second básscáth with one massive, flailing paw. The first was already dead, in a crumpled heap against the tunnel wall. The knocker turned to him, their eyes locked, and gave him a satisfied smile.

As the throng of chasing básscáth closed around him, he closed his eyes in grim acceptance. And then he was gone, swallowed by the dreadful mass of monsters.

Erik slammed the gate shut, slammed down the bolt, and slid, panting, down the solid timbers until his rump hit the cold solid floor.

He was safe. The kingdom was safe.

For now.

This door would not hold back the básscáth threat forever.

Of Older and Fouler Things

***

Nohm blinked his oversized eyes as they quickly adjusted to the darkness. His people prided their ability to see in very low light, or even no light at all. But the darkness here was absolute. He could neither see nor sense anything. No sounds, no movements, no smells.

Where was he? The last thing he remembered was... oh.

Suddenly, Nohm became aware he was not alone. There was someone else. A biggun? This one was taller than anyone he had ever met. Twice as tall, in fact, and all dressed in black robes, with a hood hiding his features.

"Hello," said the stranger, in a pleasant, warm tone.

"Hello," replied Nohm. He should feel... something. Disconcerted if not afraid, yet he felt strangely comforted by this enigmatic interloper.

And suddenly, they were no longer in absolute darkness. Their surroundings changed and, in the blink of an eye, Nohm found himself in a night-time desert, illuminated by a pale blue light, though the heavens were free of moon nor stars. The unspoiled sands stretched away in every direction, as far as the eye could see. The stranger pulled back his hood and offered Nohm a genial, benign smile.

"I am sure you have questions," he said.

"Not really," sighed Nohm.

"Really?" queried the stranger, cocking his bald head to one side. "Most who come before me require some explanation."

Nohm snorted back a half-laugh. "Oh, I know I'm dead," he shrugged. "As for what happens next... well... things cannot get worse, can they?"

"Very true," mused the stranger. "My name is Usir, Nohm. I'm here to escort you to your afterlife."

"Thank you, Usir," said Nohm. "You say it is *my* afterlife?"

"That is correct."

"Will there be digging?"

"Do you want there to be?"

"I do."

"Then there will be digging, I'm sure."

"Will my wife and children be there? I do hope so. I miss them."

"I am certain they will be waiting for you, Nohm."

"What about spiders?" Nohm shuddered. "Will there be spiders?"

"Not if you don't wish there to be."

"Good," said Nohm, visibly relieved. "I might enjoy this afterlife."

"That's what it's all about, my friend," agreed Usir. "Shall we?"

Nohm looked to his chaperone and took his offered hand. Usir smiled, then gently squeezed his companion's paw in a comforting gesture, as the pair faded to nothingness.

El Caleuche

The Realm Sea, 50 nautical miles off Glaseód's southwestern coast.

Macnia's weary eyes groaned open as he roused from fitful sleep. He rotated his head to ease the stiffness in his neck, slid his stylish, knee-high boots from the table and creaked upright on the uncomfortable wooden chair.

Mouth dry from where it had hung open as he slept, his tongue sour, Macnia swept up his silver goblet and downed the remaining, tepid dregs of Lobian red. He swilled it around his tongue before swallowing, in an attempt to wash away the foul tang.

The *Scuabtuinne's* captain rose unsteadily to his feet, staggered to the huge window that formed his stateroom's back wall, embedded in her stern, and looked out over the Realm Sea's undulating, grey surface. The sun's bulbous orange orb hovered over the far western horizon. Dammit! He must have slept away the whole day. That had become the norm in recent months: drinking heavily, sleeping more, and abdicating his duties to his first mate, Ennis. He heard the men whispering when they thought he could not see or hear. They all sensed it. Something was not right with their captain. Macnia knew it, yet he could not articulate how he felt, let alone the cause for his current malaise. He was... forlorn... miserable... constantly exhausted, and a little sick. Although, three bottles of wine and several large brandies might well have contributed to that feeling today.

In truth, the only thing of which Macnia was certain was that he was *bored*. The life of a free trader[4] was fraught with peril: hijacking other vessels to steal their merchandise, smuggling restricted wares through port to sell them to his black-market customers, evading the authorities, and the far more hazardous task of eluding rival free traders.

When he first started out in this business, the excitement was all-consuming. His life was at risk every day. He always had to stay sharp. Alert. Cognisant of danger from any avenue, including from within. Many a lesser trader had lost his command, his ship – even his life – at the hands of overly ambitious crewmates. Macnia was sure to keep a close eye on his men and only recruited those he could... trust? No, trust

---

[4] Free trader is a euphemistic name for a smuggler. Macnia and the crew of the *Scuabtuinne* specialised as Flaskers, experts in liberating high-value alcoholic consignments from legitimate traders to sell on the black market. However, Macnia took pride in his ability to obtain and move whatever cargo his clients desired.

was not the right word. Macnia trusted no-one. Predict, perhaps? Yes, that was more fitting.

However, Macnia no longer felt that exhilarating rush of danger when he pulled on his boots each morning. For one thing, he was usually still wearing them. And with increasing frequency, morning entirely passed him by. However, the main reason for his ennui was, quite simply, boredom. It had all become too easy. Back in the day, the authorities were as rough and brutal as the buccaneers they pursued. In fact, the only notable difference between brigands and the powers-that-be was the uniform they wore and the flags they flew. Why accept a bribe when law enforcement could just as easily slaughter the crew, steal their ship and cargo, and sell it on the black market themselves? But those old-school naval captains were a relic of a bygone age. Their modern replacements were equally corrupt, though easily bought-off with just a few gold coróins, or they were inept. Macnia felt that very few of his contemporaries were a real threat to him – after all, the *Scuabtuinne* was the fastest ship in the realm. No one could rival the manner in which her sleek, black hull sliced through the waves like some great shark. And no other captain could compare to Macnia's cunning and guile.

Gods, he was *bored*!

El Caleuche

Suddenly, a voice called out from the main deck, above, though the words were too indistinct to make out, followed by the sharp peeling of the helm's bell — a steady, constant rhythm calling all hands to their posts. It could only mean one thing.

A ship.

It was impossible to make out any details of the other vessel in the fading light, even with the use of his trusty brass telescope. But her style was unusual — twin-masted and multi-decked, with a distinctive sloping bow and a broad, single stern castle. She was clearly designed for speed and manoeuvrability, whilst leaving plenty of space for cargo. She was quite unlike any ship Macnia had ever seen.

"Any signs of life, Skipper?" asked Kamryn, the *Scuabtuinne's* barrelman[5].

"No movement," shrugged Macnia. "There are a couple of lamps lit amidships, so she seems to be manned. Tell me, Rat, what do you see?"

---

[5] A barrelman is the title given to a ship's chief navigator, responsible for manning the crow's nest atop her tallest mast.

Macnia trusted his navigator's keen eyes. If there was anything to see, Kamryn would spot it, which is how he earned the nickname Rat – as in eyes like a shithouse rat[6].

The barrelman raised his scope once more.

"She's not wallowing," he appraised. "Though she's sitting quite low in the water, which tells me she's well-stocked. The sails are furled, though she's not at anchor. I'm guessing they're in trouble. Oh, that's interesting…"

"What is?"

Macnia took the offered long scope from Kamryn and let his navigator align it.

"What am I looking at?" he asked.

"Her name," said Kamryn. "You ever seen anything like that?"

It came into focus, like an optical illusion; fine, gold cursive, painted on her stern's dark boards:

'El Caleuche.'

---

[6] Kamryn much preferred his self-adorned moniker: Hawk. It had never stuck with his fellow crewmates.

"What kind of language is that?" asked Kamryn, taking back the scope. "Ell Cah-looch? Ell Kai-look? How do you even say it? Where d'you think she's from, Skip?"

"Not a clue," replied Macnia, his voice far away. Because, just at that moment, he did see movement aboard the mysterious ship. He raised his telescope for a closer look as a dark figure came into view, approached the rail... and waved.

***

"You sure this is wise, Skipper?" asked Ennis, as they lowered the small boat over the *Scuabtuinne's* starboard side and into the water.

"Wise?" chuckled Macnia. "What's up with you, man? It's not like you to be so easily spooked."

"I... I don't know," replied Ennis, shiftily. "It's just... I heard all sorts of things lately."

"What things?"

"Bad things. Ships found adrift; their whole crews lost — no sign of 'em. There are some troubling things out here,

Skipper. Things we know nothing about. Things beyond our ken."

"I've met your Ken, Ennis," jibed Macnia. "There are many things beyond him – he's thick as mince!"

"Very funny, Skipper," sighed Ennis. "You know what I mean – things beyond our understanding. Terrible things."

"Look, get a grip, Ennis," said Macnia. "We *are* the terrible things on the Realm Sea! There's nothing scarier than us. If these people have any malicious intent, they'd be wise to try it on someone else."

Ennis had the good grace to look embarrassed. "So, what's the plan, Skipper?"

"I suspect our friends over there are in trouble. I'll go over, see what they need and then offer our help... for the right price, of course."

"Are you sure you don't want me to come with?" asked Ennis.

"No, you stay here and man the helm," Macnia insisted. "If they try anything, you know what to do."

"Aye, Captain."

"Now... how do I look?"

El Caleuche

"Devilishly handsome, as always, Skip," grinned Ennis.

And this much was true. Macnia had washed and changed ahead of the excursion to the stricken vessel – after all, he was known throughout the realm for his well-groomed, debonair appearance and it would not do to look as though he had just been dredged from a bilge-pump filter. He wore his favourite pantaloons – the cream ones with the double-stitched seams – black, patent leather knee-high boots, the burgundy jacket with the silver brocade on the lapel and shoulders, and a ruffed, white blouson beneath. His nails were painted to match the heavy, woollen jacket, with the same shade applied to his lips, whilst his eyes were lined black, and his mousy beard trimmed and shaped for the first time in weeks. He was perfectly aware the men thought him a dandy — not that they would ever dare say it to his face — but appearances were important to Macnia. Having grown up with nothing, it made him feel… *complete* to care about his looks. The excitement of this break from the mundane had reinvigorated him. If he was to visit this other ship, they would see the *Scuabtuinne's* captain at his most glorious, glamorous best. And if they were to cause him any trouble? Well, then they would see his darker side. Many underestimated Macnia due to his pleasant affability, and that suited him just fine. It was a mistake few ever had the opportunity to make twice.

***

"Hola, mi amigo," said the grinning sailor, reaching down to help Macnia over the rail. "Welcome aboard *El Caleuche*."

It had grown almost completely dark in the time it had taken to make the short crossing and the *Scuabtuinne* was now invisible to Macnia, even though she was at anchor just a few hundred yards away.

"Ah, so that's how you say it? *Ell Cah-lee-oo-chay*?" said Macnia, clasping the sailor's hand in both of his own and shaking it vigorously. The four crewmen he had chosen to accompany him from the *Scuabtuinne* clambered onto the deck behind. "I would never have guessed. What language is it?"

"Is Español, señor," replied the sailor, his smile faltering only slightly as a look of confusion passed over his features.

"Español?"

"Si, my name is Luis Fernando Cardenas, señor. I am *El Caleuche's* captain."

El Caleuche

Cardenas was an interesting fellow, with sparkling, soulful eyes. He wasn't overly tall, but he had the solid, muscular build common to most career seamen, accompanied with the weathered, leathery skin sported by most who worked in the open. His mane of thick, black hair was streaked with grey, and though his face was largely obscured by his thick, salt-and-pepper beard, his features were masculine and handsome enough, though his age indeterminate.

"A pleasure to meet you, Captain," said Macnia. "I am Captain Macnia of the *Scuabtuinne*. You appear to be in some sort of trouble?"

"Si, Captain Macnia. Our steering assembly is damaged. We do not have the tools to repair it, though my men endeavour to effect temporary repairs until we can find land."

"My men may be able to assist," said Macnia. "For a price, of course."

Captain Cardenas sighed yet nodded in understanding.

"Of course, Captain Macnia. We are simple traders, exporting goods out of the Chiloé Archipelago in the Americas, part of the glorious empire of España."

"Never heard of it," shrugged Macnia.

"No matter, Captain," replied Cardenas. "We would, of course, be in your debt. You are welcome to take a portion of our cargo in return for your assistance."

"And what do you have in your hold, Captain Cardenas?"

"Animal products in the main: suet, leather, dried meats. We also carry some grain, some spice, and a small amount of gold ore. You can take as much as your men can carry back to your ship."

Macnia raised an eyebrow, then nodded his agreement.

"Thank you, Captain Macnia," sighed Cardenas, his relief palpable. "My first mate, Francisco, will show your men the way."

Macnia signalled to his chief tinker, Culloch, and the handyman hefted his canvas tool bag and he and his two junior tinkers, Doyle, and Euan, followed Francisco towards the helm.

"That is a most generous offer, Captain," said Macnia.

"It is worth it, Captain Macnia. Without your kind assistance, we could remain stranded here. Or perhaps fall victim to less scrupulous seafarers who would take more than just a portion of our cargo."

Macnia had the decency to look a little embarrassed, though quickly overcame the awkward moment.

"I am just happy we came across you when we did," he said. "Another few minutes and we might not have seen you."

He looked back across the narrow stretch of water to where the *Scuabtuinne* lay hidden in the darkness. If he concentrated, he could just make out the pinprick of a couple of lamps, burning at midship in the indigo gloom, like pinholes in a dark sheet.

"Gracias Captain," said Cardenas. "I too am pleased you found us. I insist you join me for dinner."

"I would be delighted," grinned Macnia, bowing deeply. He nodded to his remaining crewman, Malky. Macnia had brought the brawny sailor mainly for protection, should they need it, but he saw no threat here.

"Malky," he said. "See if Culloch needs any help with the repairs, yes?"

"Aye, Skip," grunted Malky, eyeing their host, suspiciously. "Be careful, eh, Captain?"

"I'll be fine, Malky," Macnia assured him, patting his man's shoulder. He lowered his voice. "Keep your eyes open. Just in case, eh?"

Malky nodded, scowling at Cardenas before trudging towards the helm, following the others.

"Shall we, Captain?" said Cardenas, gesturing towards belowdecks.

"Lead on, Captain," grinned Macnia.

***

Malky caught up with Culloch and the others just as they arrived at the helm. The tinker prodded at the large wooden-spoked wheel, turning it this way and that, grunting, as though lost in thought.

"What's up?" Malky asked him, though the tinker did not answer, which was not particularly unusual. Culloch was a man of few words – gruff, bordering on rude – though he was an excellent tinker. The best handyman Malky had ever been crewed with in all his years at sea, Culloch had saved their skins more times than he cared to count. For that reason, the

Scuabtuinne's crew could easily forgive the tinker's peculiar, misanthropic foibles.

With the customary grunt well known to all men of a certain age, Culloch clambered to his knees, holding his lamp near the helm's base, and peered into the darkness.

"Can we get down below?" he asked their guide. "I need to take a closer look."

Francisco nodded and begrudgingly unhooked a huge bunch of keys from his belt. He slotted it into a hidden lock in the helm's plinth and twisted the key. It gave a muffled clunk as the latch disengaged, then he raised the recessed iron loop handle and hauled the trapdoor open with a teeth-gritting groan.

Malky held his lamp over the chamber and squinted into the darkness. He exchanged looks with Culloch.

"Well? What you bloody waiting for?" scowled the tinker. "An invitation from the king?"

With an impatient sigh, Francisco barged past them, snatched the lamp from Malky's hand and traipsed down the creaking wooden steps. The four *Scuabtuinne* crewmen followed.

The staircase was only short and the space below was not even high enough to properly stand without cracking your head on the beams above. There was only sufficient room for the four of them to assemble.

"Hey, where'd he go?" asked Culloch shining their remaining lamp around the tiny enclosure. Francisco had vanished.

Just then, the hatchway slammed shut, showering them with dust, and the lock clunked with an ominous clang.

***

El Caleuche's stateroom lacked the grandeur of Macnia's own, though it was roomy and opulent, with walnut-panelled walls and an ornate, mahogany dining table with twelve matching chairs. Comfortable, warm light flickered from the wall sconces and the silver candelabra that dominated the table's centrepiece. A team of stewards scurried around the table, pouring drinks, with still more bringing food from the galley. Macnia was baffled by the sheer number of staff that seemed to be below decks on *El Caleuche*. He had seen dozens of them on the short walk from the main deck.

Macnia was not Cardenas's only guest this evening, though the massive table was not even close to full capacity. They were joined by three others: a tall, elegant, almost impossibly handsome man, with an equally beautiful woman sat at each side.

"Captain Macnia, allow me to introduce my guests: Lord Pincoy of Chiloé and his charming sisters, Pincoya and Chilota."

"A pleasure to meet you," said Macnia, beaming his most beguiling smile. He offered his hand to Pincoya, the nearest sister, but she simply looked at it, eyeing him suspiciously.

"And who is this?" Pincoy asked Cardenas without taking his cold eyes from Macnia. The lord's accent was thick, yet it dripped with the haughty privilege and disdain of the highborn. Macnia had met his kind before. He had tossed more than one such arrogant aristocrat overboard before now for such a show of supercilious scorn and had not lost a wink of sleep over it.

"Apologies, my lord," grovelled Cardenas. "Our ship has run into some difficulty and Captain Macnia here has kindly offered his men's services to repair the damage. I thank the lord they found us when they did."

Pincoy still had not removed his sneering gaze from Macnia, though he seemed to grudgingly accept Cardenas's explanation and his fierce expression softened somewhat.

"So, you are our hero, Captain Macnia?" said the sister known as Chilota. She smiled, blushing coquettishly, seemingly more welcoming of the newcomer than her siblings.

"Hero?" chuckled Macnia. "That is, perhaps, a little strong. I am happy to offer my services to any fellow voyager, as I would hope they would do for me."

"Well, I, for one, am grateful for your benevolence, Captain," said Chilota. "And I welcome your presence too – the company of my siblings and Captain Cardenas has become somewhat tiresome on this tedious, seemingly endless voyage."

She giggled, fluttering her eyes at Macnia, whilst Pincoya rolled hers and took a deep gulp of her wine.

"Oh, really, Chilota," she growled. "Show some decorum."

The aristocratic trio were very... *different*. The family resemblance was undeniable; each with the same high cheekbones, large, silvern eyes, aquiline nose, and long face. They shared identical dark-brown hair; needle-straight and pulled into a four-strand braid, woven with the finest chains of precious metals and delicate jewels. Their skin was pale, with an almost greenish hue, whilst their ears were slightly pointed. They looked almost elvish.

"Hush now, sister," tutted Chilota. "Captain Macnia does not mind, do you?"

"Of course not, ma'am," he answered.

"See? Now pull the stick out of your backside and stop making our guest feel so uncomfortable. Can you do that?"

Pincoy shot his sister a glare, and she demurred, just for a moment. However, her words seemed to resonate with him and, when he turned back to Macnia, his demeanour thawed entirely.

"Tell me, Captain Macnia," he said. "What is it you and your crew do?"

"I am in… transit," Macnia replied. "Supply and demand. I source items of value to my clientele's specification and move them to wherever they need to be."

"Supply of what?" Pincoy probed.

"Whatever my clients require," he answered, evasively. "I do not ask too many questions. I just ensure I obtain whatever they need."

"You're a brigand," sneered Pincoya. She was making a statement, not asking a question.

Macnia shrugged, grinning in mischief.

"I don't set too much stock in labels," he said. "I prefer to call myself a free trader."

"You're a pirate!"

"Sister, please!" snapped her brother. "Do not be so discourteous to our guest. Captain Macnia is rescuing our stranded vessel. Who are we to judge how a man might make his living?"

"A living preying on others?" snarled Pincoya.

"We all do what we must, sister," giggled Chilota. "Captain Macnia and his men are no different, I'm sure. Besides, I find him quite charming."

Macnia smiled as a steward placed a bowl before him of pale broth with large pieces of fish and vegetables floating in it. His stomach growled as the rich fragrance wafted to his nostrils. Macnia could not recall the last time he had eaten a proper meal, but he waited for the other guests to start before taking up his spoon and tucking into the dish. It was wonderful –bursting with flavour – and he shovelled down several ravenous spoonfuls before looking up at the other guests, all of whom watched him with amusement.

"Please excuse me," he said. "This is quite delicious, Captain Cardenas. My compliments to your cook."

"Thank you, Captain," nodded Cardenas. "We are blessed to have him."

The following courses were equally excellent – sea bream, garnished with lemon and parsley, accompanied by baby potatoes, roasted carrots and tenderstem broccoli. A fish pie, topped with creamed potatoes, and finished with a light dessert, consisting of sponge fingers soaked in some kind of liqueur, topped with thick, whipped vanilla cream and dusted with bitter, powdered chocolate that perfectly complimented the cream's sweetness. And the wine... the wine! Macnia usually favoured full, fruity reds, but this crisp, dry white was wonderful. After several glasses, he felt more than a little light-headed.

After an admittedly inauspicious start, his fellow guests had proven themselves quite delightful company. Pincoy was witty, sharp, and interesting, whilst Chilota continued to flirt shamelessly. Cardenas was Macnia's kind of companion too – a fellow seasoned sailor, full of witty anecdotes, and clearly devoted to his ship and her crew. He treated his stewards with kind dignity and respect, thanking them each time they refilled his glass or bussed away his dish. That told Macnia everything he needed to know about *El Caleuche's* skipper. He believed you should always judge a man by how he treats those others would deem inferior to him rather than how he treats his peers or superiors. And it was clear that *El Caleuche's* stewards cherished their captain, just as Macnia knew his crew respected him.

Only Pincoya seemed immune to Macnia's charms, though her barbs became less pointed as the evening went on, even if her expression suggested the wine was too sour for her tastes. Macnia suspected that, while the sister's antipathy was due to his presence, her demeanour would have been no different in any other company. After a while, Pincoya's manner changed entirely. Her body language softened, becoming coy and flirtatious. She even took the wine bottle from the steward and refilled Macnia's chalice herself. She dipped her finger in his drink and swirled it, smiling coquettishly, before sucking her finger dry, her eyes locked with his the whole time.

"So, tell me, Pincoy," Macnia asked, desperate to disengage from the uncomfortable dalliance, "to where are you and your delightful sisters headed, my friend?" He took a deep swig from his wine.

Pincoy smiled, somewhat enigmatically. "Ah, our friend, Captain Cardenas, kindly offered to grant us passage to the old world. We have *so* longed to see it."

"The old world?" Macnia slurred. It was not a phrase he was familiar with.

"Si," offered Cardenas. "Europa, the Africas, Asia."

"Yes," confirmed Pincoy, raising his chalice. "Our little slice of the world was so small. We longed to see more. To experience the world! A man such as yourself must understand, yes, Captain Macnia?"

"Um, yes, of course," garbled Macnia. His head swam, struggling to focus. Those places meant nothing to him – he had never heard of them. Right now, he was preoccupied that his tongue seemed numb and oversized, making it difficult to form cogent words. The wine must be stronger than he expected, even for a seasoned drinker like Macnia.

"Are you feeling okay, Captain Macnia?" said Pincoya, grinning slyly.

"Um. 'M 'kay," he managed. Something about the sister's expression disconcerted him.

"Wha' you done t'me?" Macnia slurred, attempting to climb, unsteadily to his feet. His legs gave way and he collapsed, cracking his temple against the dining table on his way down.

As Macnia's world faded, the siblings' peered down at him with expressions of amusement. They seemed... different... alien... Their features were sharper, eyes larger, more bulbous, their fingers almost claw-like. Their skin appeared... scaly. Reptilian? No... *piscine*. He even thought he could see ridges – somewhat like gills – in their slender necks. Before Macnia could digest what his eyes were seeing, the darkness engulfed him. The corona of blackness closed in from his vision's periphery as the *Scuabtuinne's* captain slipped into the void's sweet embrace.

El Caleuche

***

"This makes no sense," muttered Culloch, prodding at the steering mechanism with his penknife.

"What doesn't?" groaned Malky from his position at the foot of the steps, his head in his hands. They had tried everything to get out in the last hour but to no avail.

"This!" snapped Culloch. "I mean, this ship is… I dunno… odd? It's like a bloody antique – not seen anything like it in a dog's age. However, the timbers are all solid, not even a sign of rot."

"Okay, it's a well-tended ship," shrugged Malky, irritably. "So's the *Scuabtuinne*. What of it?"

"Yes, but look at this," cried Culloch holding up the blackened, tattered remains of something long and fibrous.

"What is it?" asked Doyle, earning himself a sharp look from the master tinker.

"Think, lad!" snapped Culloch. "How does the steering mechanism work, eh?"

"Um," ventured Euan, raising a tentative hand.

"Go on," urged Culloch.

"The wheel is attached to the tiller by means of a line[7]?" he said.

"You askin' me or tellin' me, lad?" growled the tinker.

"Um… telling you? I think."

Culloch sighed, shaking his head, irascibly. "Well, at least one of you has been paying attention," he muttered, then turned to Malky once more. "He's right. The line runs down through here from either side of the helm and through these ginnels to the tiller assembly at the stern. As you turn the wheel, the line moves the rudder to steer the ship."

"And?" shrugged Malky.

"Well, if the line gets damaged, we lose steering," Culloch told him. "And we have to repair it or replace it with fresh rope. That's what I expected to find down here."

"So, you're telling me they cut it themselves?" asked Malky, not grasping what the tinker was getting at.

---

[7] In nautical circles, a 'line' refers to a rope.

"No! That's just it," exclaimed Culloch. "This line wasn't cut. It *rotted*. And judging by the state of the ginnel grooves this steering mechanism hasn't worked in bloody years. Decades, even."

"Then how could they steer the ship?" asked Malky, his brow creased in confusion.

"You tell me. There's no way this ship has moved in a long time. Not with steering, at least."

Just then, the hatchway swung open again and Malky jumped to his feet, narrowly avoiding braining himself on the thick beam above. A crossbow pointed through the trapdoor, held by Francisco.

"Out," grunted *El Caleuche's* first mate, gesturing with the bow.

As he mounted the stairs and emerged onto the deck, Malky gasped. They were surrounded by sailors of all shapes, sizes, and skin colours, some dressed in fine, exotic garb, others in tattered rags. The more raggedy souls appeared... drained... emaciated. Their eyes sunken and skin pallid, washed out, hanging from their skeletons like ill-fitting suits. There must have been *hundreds* of them – more than this ship should feasibly be able to hold. And they all looked... haunted.

The weight of their misery poured from them, threatening to engulf Malky... he felt the cold feeling of dread in his chest, his breath catching in his lungs as an involuntary sob escaped his lips. What had happened to these poor souls?

"What *are* you...?"

The crowd of sailors parted, and through their ranks stepped three newcomers – a man and two women. At least, that is how they appeared to Malky, though something about them did not feel right. They were tall, graceful, moving with the poise and grace of dancers, almost flowing between *El Caleuche's* crew. Their garb was sophisticated and refined, made from elegant, aquamarine silks that left little to the imagination. Their beautiful features seemed to shift in the moonlight like a pearlescent optical illusion: one moment their visage appeared attractive, alluring, but then, as they caught the light differently, they seemed almost monstrous and eerily peculiar.

The smaller of the sisters stepped away from the group and sauntered towards the *Scuabtuinne* crewmen, an enticing smile playing upon her ruby lips.

"Hello," she cooed, as she circled them, in much the same way as a cat might torment a mouse. "You are the kind saviours who have come to mend our ship? Our rescuers? Such fine figures of men." She stroked Malky's stubbled cheeky, playfully, lingering for a moment, standing far too close to the veteran sailor for his comfort. He gulped, fighting back the urge to scurry for a hiding place.

"Who... who are you?" he managed.

"I am Chilota," she replied, cheerfully. "And this is my brother, Pincoy and sister, Pincoya."

"*What* are you?" Malky gasped, recovering his senses.

"Enough of this," snapped Pincoya. "Don't play with your food, sister."

"Now, now, Pincoya," chided Chilota. "Patience, sister. I am just talking with our friend... I'm sorry, what was your name?"

"Um... Malky," he replied, though his rodent hindbrain screamed at him, demanding to know what the other one meant about "food".

"Malky! What a delightful name," Chilota cried, gleefully. "I am just talking with Malky and his wonderful, sweet, and not at all roguish friends. After all, they were kind enough to come to our aid."

"Where is our captain?" growled Culloch. "If you've hurt him—"

"You'll do what?" sneered Pincoy. "What do you think you could do to us, fat little man?"

Culloch, for once, had the good sense to hold his tongue. Malky sensed this man – if he *was* a man – could end them all without so much as breaking a sweat. He was slender and rangy, with well-toned muscles that bulged through his garments' wispy silks.

"Perhaps our new friends need a demonstration of what happens to those who defy us, brother?" chirped Chilota. Pincoy grinned and nodded in curt agreement.

Chilota turned back to Malky, smiling sweetly, her big, argent eyes locked with his, drawing him in, filling his world. He felt powerless to resist as she leaned forward and kissed him, tenderly on the lips. When she pulled away again, her beautiful, impish features were gone, replaced with something truly horrifying. Some sort of fish-like creature: its eyes too big, yet the same shade of pale silver, its skin, tinged green, and scaled lips twisted into a cruel smile. Malky gasped and tried to back away, but the creature lashed out a clawed hand, burying its fingers deep in his chest. Malky grunted, unable to catch his breath. He clutched at its hand, attempting to yank it free from his ribcage, but the beast was too strong – its grip like a vice around his heart. He felt a numbing cold begin to spread out from his rib cage, as his arms grew weak, and his vision blurred, and his head began to swim. Malky slumped to his knees. He tried in vain to gulp down lungfuls of breath, where they caught in his paralysed throat.

As Malky felt the final residues of consciousness drain from him, his focus crumbling and the world fading to blackness, he heard Chilota's honied voice whisper in his ear: "Thank you, my darling."

***

Macnia lurched awake, his pounding head span and his mind raced as it tried to make sense of his surroundings or recall how he came to be there. His stomach churned, filled with the green-gilled nausea of a heavy drinking session. He was in total darkness.

Light burst into the room, searing his vision, accompanied by the groaning of old hinges, but his efforts to shield his eyes were hampered by the shackles around his wrists.

"What...?" he grumbled, as a figure slipped through the pool of blinding light and crouched at his side.

"Hush now, Captain Macnia," whispered Cardenas. "We do not have very long."

El Caleuche's captain busied himself lighting a small oil lamp then, as its warm, orange glow filled the room, he began unlocking Macnia's irons.

"What's going on?" slurred Macnia. "Where am I?"

"Drink this," insisted Cardenas, thrusting a leather flask into Macnia's hands. Its pouch was warm to the touch.

"What is it?"

"Just drink. It will help you feel better."

Macnia did as he was told and took a large draw from the flask. Its contents were sharp, bitter, and brackish, yet accompanied by a sweet, warming aftertaste that spread through his chest and ignited his synapses.

"It is black tea, sweetened with honey and laced with a little rum," Cardenas explained. "It helps counteract the poison."

"Poison?" said Macnia, his fogged brain lost in a miasma of confusion. Then it all came flooding back. "The siblings… your guests."

"Not my guests," snarled Cardenas. "My gaolers."

"What *are* they?"

"They are the sirena chiloté – ancient, cruel, and terrible rulers of the Chiloé seas. They beguile us with beautiful visions, though beneath their masks hide monsters – horrifying creatures from beneath the sea. They are feared and worshipped as gods by the Chiloén locals. I believed them nought more than folk legends until I too fell victim to them. They posed as dignitaries, seeking passage to the old world, just as they told you. Soon after we left port, their true nature was revealed."

"And they poisoned me?" asked Macnia. "Was it the food?"

"No. Their talons secrete a venom that paralyses their victims whilst they feed on their essence," Cardenas explained. "When Pincoya stirred your wine with her finger—"

Macnia groaned. How could he have been so stupid, to lower his guard and allow himself to fall victim to a predator?

"The chiloté seized my ship long ago, Captain," Cardenas continued. "They forced me to do their bidding and I am ashamed to say I have been in their employ for longer than I care to remember – perhaps hundreds of years. As we encounter other vessels, we appear to be stricken and in need of help. When they come to our aid, Pincoy and his sisters ambush their sailors and keep them here as prisoners forevermore."

"Why?"

"They feed on us – on our lifeforce. They drain us dry until there is nothing left. It is how they stay young and vital. They spare me that fate as long as I play along with their deception."

Macnia clambered to his feet, ducking his head to avoid the beams in the low-ceilinged brig and massaging life back into his wrists. "I must return to my ship."

"I will do all I can to assist you, Captain," said Cardenas. "But the chiloté should not be taken lightly. They are strong, cunning, and vicious. It will not be easy."

"I must form a plan," mused Macnia. "How many souls are aboard *El Caleuche*, Captain Cardenas? If we band together, surely we can overpower the sirens and we can all break free?"

Cardenas smiled, though it contained not a trace of humour, and snorted through his nostrils, shaking his head regretfully.

"I'm not sure you understand, Captain," said Cardenas, his head bowed, a tear rolling down his cheek until it became lost in his bushy beard. "It is too late for me and the others. And it will soon be too late for you. Each sunrise, *El Caleuche* fades from existence and reappears... somewhere else. Sometimes I do not even know the stars. Like here... it is like another world. We are eternally lost at sea. And as each new sun shines upon her, and *El Caleuche* disappears, all souls aboard become enslaved to her. They become part of her crew, destined to remain with her, party to the hideous subterfuge of the sirena for all time. What is worse, we are unable to take up arms against the chiloté. We are no longer alive, Captain. I have been long dead. You marvelled at how many crewmates you have seen below *El Caleuche's* decks, Captain Macnia? Yet you have seen just a tiny proportion of her crew. We number in the *thousands*, our crew consisting of all the poor souls who fell afoul of our captors. And we remain until *they* are finished with us. Until they have drained our lifeforce to nothingness, at which point we cease to exist."

Macnia's heart pounded in his chest, his scalp crawling as he listened to Cardenas' terrible tale.

"There… there must be something we can do?" he floundered.

"I fear not. However, I can no longer be a part of this terrible charade. I will do what I can to aid the escape of you and your men. One of your number has perished already, but the others are safe… for now."

"What? Who?"

"I am sorry, I do not know their names, Captain," Cardenas admitted. "But we have little time. You have perhaps an hour before sunrise to return to the safety of your ship. I will help you… though I want something in return."

"What do you want?" asked Macnia, though he knew the answer before Cardenas uttered the words.

"Free us, Captain Macnia. Let us be at peace. Kill the chiloté."

***

Macnia forced his shoulder against the heavy spar that barred the hold's double doors. It slowly inched from the iron brackets until it finally popped free, and he hefted the unwieldly timber and carefully placed it on the deck before hauling the doors open. Inside, Culloch, Euan, and Doyle blinked and shielded their eyes as they tried to focus.

"Captain?" enquired Culloch, but Macnia quietened him by raising a finger to his lips. He beckoned for them to follow, and they clambered up the rickety wooden staircase until they emerged on the aft deck.

"What's going on?" hissed the old tinker.

"Malky?" asked Macnia, but Culloch's sorrowful headshake confirmed his worse fears.

"We're getting out of here," Macnia told him, handing them each a short sword. "But first, we have a job to do."

Euan and Doyle shared fearful glances and turned their imploring eyes towards their mentor.

"No way, Captain," said Culloch, folding his arms in uncompromising fashion and refusing to accept the proffered sword. "We've seen these... *things* in action. There's no way we're taking them on. Let's just get our boat and get the hells out of here."

"I… I can't do that," said Macnia. "I made a promise, Culloch, and my word is my bond. However, you are right; I cannot ask you to risk yourself for a bargain I made. You three should go. Take the boat and get back to the *Scuabtuinne*. I'll do what needs to be done and then I'll follow on."

"We can't leave you behind, Skipper," argued Culloch.

"Of course you can! Besides, it wasn't a request; it was an order. Get yourself out of here before they realise we're free."

"There's too many of 'em, Captain," said the tinker. "More'n I've ever seen on a single ship before. Even *you* can't fight 'em all."

"I don't need to," Macnia told him. "I'm doing this *for* them. I just need to take down the three siblings – they're behind all this. The crew won't get in my way. Now go! I won't tell you again."

He thrust the sword into Culloch's hands and clasped them, just for a few moments, exchanging expressions of camaraderie that mere words could not convey. Macnia fumbled at the flask tied to his belt and handed it to Culloch.

"Here. Take this."

"What is it?"

"Some kind of tea," Macnia told him. "If you run into those… things… if they scratch you, it may help. I don't know – take it, just in case."

"What about you, Skipper?"

"Culloch, I'll be fine! You know me, man. Many have tried to kill me, but none have succeeded. Now, I'm trusting you to get these young lads back home, okay?"

"Come on," said Culloch, eventually, reluctantly breaking away and leading his apprentices to the side rail, where their rowboat was tied up below. When they had disappeared from view, Macnia hefted his sword, his jaw set in determination, and headed below decks.

***

"I think what Pincoya is saying, is that perhaps you acted in haste, sister," sighed Pincoy, stepping between his bickering sisters and pushing them apart.

"Haste?" snarled Pincoya. "She's a greedy little bitch, that's what she is! That big one could have fed the three of us for weeks."

"It was a show of force!" screeched Chilota. "He was their strongest fighter. I could sense his intention. He would have turned on us at his first opportunity."

"What say you, Captain?" asked Pincoy of Cardenas. *El Caleuche's* captain sat in his armchair by the wood-burning stove, staring into the middle distance and paying the squabbling chiloté no heed.

"Hmmm?" he murmured, roused from his reverie.

"My sister's actions earlier? Do you feel she did the right thing? Would these men have attacked us?"

"Probably," shrugged Cardenas. "The sea breeds hard men. They tend to lash out when cornered."

"See?" hissed Chilota, victoriously. "Even Cardenas agrees. Thank you, Captain."

"You did not let me finish, my lady," said Cardenas. "You have not encountered men like these before. They are dangerous. Perhaps as dangerous as you."

"We have dealt with brigands before," sneered Pincoya. "In the end, they all fall to their knees."

"Not like these men," pushed Cardenas. "Most pirates are individuals, with loyalty to none but themselves. These men love their captain, their crew, their ship. They would kill for one another. They would *die* for one another! And with men like this, the only thing more dangerous than earning their ire is to harm one of their number. Their vengeance knows no bounds. It is second only to their survival instinct. They will not go down without a fight."

Chilota threw her arms in the air in petulant fashion and stormed across the stateroom, throwing herself onto a chaise long with the air of a sulking teenager.

"No matter," said Pincoy. "It will soon be sunrise and then they will be ours. Keep them locked away until then."

A knock on the cabin door made them all spin around.

"I ordered that we not be disturbed, Captain," snapped Pincoy. Cardenas simply gave a nonchalant shrug in response.

"Answer it, sister," Pincoy instructed Pincoya.

"Answer it?" she snarled. "Do I look like the help?"

"You are nearest. Just answer the damned door!"

With a peevish sigh, Pincoya stormed to the door and yanked it open. There was nobody there.

"Hello?" she said, poking her head out into the corridor. She recoiled, stumbling backwards into the stateroom, and landing on her backside, narrowly avoiding having her head cleaved off by the sweeping sword blade beyond. A crimson gash in her brow was testament to how close she came to decapitation. They heard fleeing footsteps on the corridor's deck boards.

"Sister? Are you okay?" gasped Chilota, rushing to Pincoya's side.

"Who was it?" demanded Pincoya

"Macnia!" she growled.

Macnia sprinted for mid-deck, clearing the steps in twos as he burst into the cool night air. He could feel the chiloté in close pursuit.

He leapt the narrow line he had stretched across the doorway, hovering just a few inches above the ground, snatched up the burning lamp he had left nearby and turned to face his chasers.

Pincoya was first through the door, driven by vengeance, just as Macnia expected. Truth be told, he did not expect it to be so easy as to take her head off in that way, but he needed to make the chiloté mad. Angry people made mistakes. Whether the same could be said of these creatures, Macnia did not know – he could only hope.

Sure enough, Pincoya's foot caught the trip line, bringing down the bucket of oil Macnia had carefully positioned above the doorway. It doused her, making her gasp as the pungent liquid ran down her body, soaking her to the skin. Before she could react, Macnia hurled the lamp at her feet, where it smashed, immediately engulfing Pincoya in a ball of white-hot flame. She staggered, flailing her arms, screaming in agony, setting light to everything she touched, until she collapsed in a burning heap. In moments, there was no more movement from her.

"Sister!" cried Chilota. She launched herself at Macnia, every vestige of human glamour disappeared; all teeth and talons and burning vengeance. As Macnia had hoped, anger inspired haste, and Chilota had no mind for her safety. Macnia thrust his sword towards her chest, but the siren was quick and agile and, although she dodged his blade, it still pierced her shoulder, driving deep into flesh and bone. She screeched in pain and fell, writhing, to the floor. She crawled away, desperate to escape Macnia's furious vengeance.

"Enough!" roared Pincoy, stepping through the doorway and onto the deck, where one sister lay dead, the other gravely wounded. Around them, the fire began to spread, flames licking hungrily at the dry timbers.

Pincoy's glamour had also dropped, and his visage was more fearsome than either of his sisters. He had the appearance of something that lived in the darkest depths of the sea, preying on those beasts brave or foolhardy enough to venture into their lagoons. He was the creature that hid in the trenches that even the fiercest sharks warned their pups to avoid.

"Humans!" he snarled. "My people have ruled the seas for millennia! And then *you* came along. Humans, with your ships, and your cannons, and your swords. And now you think you can murder my sister and just walk away?"

Pincoy drew his own sword – a long, slim, flattened blade, almost like an epee, though one that appeared to be made from some form of blackened glass. It looked sharp enough to make the air bleed. He flicked it across the space between them, creating a piercing, whipping sound.

"Oh, I'm not walking anywhere, Pincoy," said Macnia. "For one thing, it's a little too wet, don't you think? I'd probably sink. But only probably – I'm quite light on my feet."

"What?" said Pincoy, confused.

"The sea?" explained Macnia. "It's quite difficult to walk on."

"Enough of this!" growled the siren king. "Enough of you and your... words! Now I kill you."

"You can try."

"I *will* try. And I will succeed."

"Not if I succeed first."

"That goes without saying."

"But I did say it."

"And so did I."

"Wait... what?" said Macnia. "No, you didn't."

"I... um... Oh, to hell with this! Now you die, *pirate*."

Pincoy lunged at Macnia, the slim blade headed straight for his heart, forcing the buccaneer to parry it away with his short sword's edge. Macnia grasped Pincoy's vest and pulled him close until their faces were so near that he could smell the chiloté's fishy breath.

"I *hate* it when people call me that," snarled Macnia. "I'm not a pirate, I'm a bloody free trader."

He pushed Pincoy back and delivered a sweeping, diagonal downward cut, which the siren easily blocked.

And whilst they fought, *El Caleuche* burned.

Ducking beneath another deadly, horizontal slash, Macnia narrowly avoided Pincoy's blade once more but felt the rush of air as it whooshed by his face.

"Is that all you've got?" he grinned, with false bravado. "You'll have to do better than that if you want me to join your floating lunchbox."

"Oh, that is no longer an option, pirate," the siren snarled. "I just want you dead!"

In truth, Macnia feared his opponent's prowess as a fighter. Pincoy was taller, stronger, and a much more accomplished swordsman. He was clearly well trained, whereas Macnia had learned to fight by simply not dying for a long time and had the scars to prove it.

However, Macnia had not survived a long, hazardous career on the high seas for no good reason. He had fought many fine swordsmen down the years, and they all had one thing in common: they fought with honour. Now, whilst Macnia did have an honour of sorts, it was highly flexible. He had a motto: if in doubt, cheat.

At the end of the next flurry of engagement, Macnia seized Pincoy once more and pulled him close, preventing his opponent from swinging his sword.

"Did you hear that?" he hissed, as the pair wrestled in close quarters.

"What?" asked a nonplussed Pincoy.

"This."

Macnia lunged at Pincoy and clamped his teeth around the siren's fleshy earlobe. Pincoy screeched in pain as Macnia bit down hard and wrenched, tearing away a chunk of flesh and cartilage and spat the foul-tasting morsel onto the deck. As Macnia released him, Pincoy staggered backwards, clutching his agonised ear. Before the siren could recover his composure, Macnia seized his moment. He stomped down on Pincoy's ankle, which gave way with a satisfying snap. He batted the elegant blade from the chiloté's hand, then thrust his shortsword upwards, through the siren's throat until its momentum was only stopped when it met skullbone. Pincoy's eyes rolled into the back of his head, and he was gone.

Macnia wrenched his sword free and let the siren's body slump to the deck. Then he cast his eyes about the burning deck, looking for Chilota, but she was nowhere to be seen.

Cardenas stepped through the doorway to join him on the deck.

"Where is she?" Macnia growled.

"It does not matter," urged *El Caleuche's* captain. "You must go."

"No, I made a promise," insisted Macnia.

"And you held true to it," smiled Cardenas. "The ship is lost. She will soon be gone, and my crew and I will go to our rest. I *feel* it. Gracias, mi amigo."

Cardenas offered his hand and Macnia took it, clasping it warmly.

"And thank you, captain," Macnia said. "You freed me. You didn't have to."

"And you freed me – you freed *all* of us. It took me a long time, but I finally did the right thing, eh? Now, you do not have much time. You must go."

Macnia turned to the eastern horizon, where the first glimmer of sunlight manifested over the world's edge. He turned back to Cardenas and nodded, as one master sailor to another, then sprinted for the port rail, which was immersed in flame. He vaulted it and dove into the Realm Sea's chilly waters below. Macnia emerged, gasping from the cold and began swimming. He could not see his ship, though she was out there, not too far away. He could *feel* her calling to him.

Defying his burning muscles, Macnia powered on, desperate to return to the comfort and safety of his beloved ship. And there she was – or, at least, her silhouette – bobbing at anchor just a few hundred yards away, made visible by the tepid, morning light. He redoubled his speed. He was nearly home.

Just then, something grabbed Macnia's ankle. Something strong. He tried in vain to break free, but its grip was vice-like. He floundered, kicking out at his subaqueous assailant, flailing his arms to stay afloat. However, he was powerless to prevent it dragging him beneath the surface and Macnia was just able to gulp a lungful of air before he was submerged.

As his eyes adjusted to the gloom, Macnia could see the reason for his current predicament. It was Chilota – her ichthyic features a mask of furious vengeance. One hand gripped Macnia's ankle as she dragged him deeper beneath the surface, before lashing out with her injured right arm and burying her claws in his left thigh. It was all Macnia could do to resist the instinct to cry out and release the precious, life-giving oxygen. He clutched at his excruciated thigh, lungs burning as the siren dragged him down, down, down. Numbness began to spread from his leg, slowly dispersing through his body. As it gripped his chest, he exhaled, sleepily, sending a plume of bubbles fleeting for the surface. His vision blurred and the darkness began to consume him. We welcomed it. Embraced it. It was so… comforting... so peaceful. All he needed to do was open his mouth, let the water in and it would all be done. He could rest.

As his vision began to fade, he looked down once more upon Chilota, her piscine lips twisted into a malevolent, triumphant grin. She had won.

Suddenly, something flashed past Macnia's shoulder, sparking him into wakefulness. He watched in astonishment as the long, slim object pierced Chilota's face, which erupted in a cloud of red mist. The harpoon had skewered her skull, protruding through one oversized eye and out the other side. Her grip relaxed and she fell away, falling into the darkness below like a dead weight.

Filled with a sudden desire to live, Macnia attempted to kick his legs, to push for the surface, but he had no more energy. His body had failed him at the last. He was finished.

Just as Macnia succumbed to his fate, he felt an arm close around his chest. Was it another of the chiloté? Were they still alive – back to exact their revenge? He was powerless to resist his assailant's tug as they began to pull him further into the briny depths.

As he slipped from the conscious world, Macnia was vaguely aware that instead of growing darker, the surrounding water had become brighter, before the blackness consumed him.

***

El Caleuche

There was only darkness. Not the blackness typical of an absence of light, but something far more palpable. It was an absence of... anything.

Macnia attempted to blink though felt nothing, and there was certainly no change to the perception of his, for want of a better word, environment. He tried to speak, and no sound came out. He tried to feel his body, and there was no sensation of touch.

Suddenly, as though someone switched on a light, Macnia found himself in a night-time desert, illuminated by some unseen blueish light. The unspoiled white sands stretched in every direction as far as the eye could see, whilst the black sky was punctuated only by the twinkling of unfamiliar constellations. There was no wind, not even a gentle breeze. There was no chill, no warmth, no sensation of any kind.

But Macnia was not alone. At his side stood a tall, robed being, his physique slender and demeanour calm. He – if he was, in fact, a *he* – stared into the middle distance, his features hidden by his hood. Macnia felt no fear, no panic. His silent companion was strangely pleasant company.

After several minutes of hushed peace, Macnia felt compelled to speak with the lofty stranger.

"So, this is it, then?" he ventured.

"This is what?" asked the stranger. He spoke in a rich, comforting tone.

"The end?" shrugged Macnia.

"Oh, it's certainly *an* end," admitted the stranger. He reached up and pulled back his hood, revealing pleasant, benign features, brown eyes filled with compassion, and his head shaved smooth. Even in this light, Macnia could make out that the man's ebony skin was crisscrossed with horrific scars; to his neck, his ears, his wrists – anywhere visible beneath those black robes. It was as though this patchwork man had been stitched together and sported the blemishes to prove it.

"Who are you?" asked Macnia.

"I have many names, Captain Macnia of the *Scuabtuinne*," grinned the man. "Osiris, Erebus, Hades, Hephaestus, Thanatos, the Grim Reaper, even just plain ol' Death. Though my mother called me Usir. Stories of me abound in the worlds of man, though they are each subtly incorrect."

"You know me?" gasped Macnia.

"I know all people," said Usir. "Eventually, at least."

"Then it's true," sighed Macnia. "I'm dead?"

"Whatever gave you that idea?" chuckled Usir.

"Um... the fact that I'm here. In the afterlife."

"Oh, this is not the afterlife," Usir told him. "This is the place that exists between the physical world and perpetuity – my unchanging domain. All come here so I can guide them on their way, wherever that may be."

Macnia bowed his head, stifling the urge to cry. There was so much he was yet to do. He had taken life for granted – drinking his time away, allowing boredom and lethargy to fester and poison his soul. He had so many regrets.

"And what awaits me on the other side, Usir?" he asked.

"That I do not know," Usir told him. "Your afterlife is for you, and you alone, to know. When the time is right, you will forge your path – I will simply show you the way and open the door. The rest is up to you."

"What? Wait…" said Macnia, confused. "Are you saying it's *not* my time?" He felt that, should his heart still be beating, it would be pounding in his chest right now.

"No, your world is not yet done with you, Captain Macnia," smiled the benevolent lord of the underworld. "You still have an important role to play."

"What? You can see my future?"

"I see all things: all possibilities, past, present, and future. My perception of time is very different to those of mortals."

"Then, can you tell me anything important? What must I do next?"

"That I cannot tell you. Not that it would make a difference: when you return to the world of the living, you will not remember meeting me."

"But… we will meet again?"

"Inevitably," grinned Usir, as the desert faded to darkness once more.

***

Macnia awoke, coughing and spluttering as the sharp tang of saltwater spewed from his lips. He felt someone roll him onto his side and the grainy roughness of wooden planks against his cheek as he vomited foul saline from his burning throat and lungs.

"He's okay," sighed a relieved, familiar voice. "Come on, skipper, sit up. Drink some of this."

Still dazed and unaware of his surroundings, Macnia allowed himself to be manhandled into a seated position, where another of his mystery companions pressed something to his lips. Something bitter, though not unpleasant, flooded over his tongue, leaving a sweet aftertaste once swallowed. He took several more sips and could feel the warmth returning to his limbs as his brain fog began to dissipate and his eyes refocussed. He was sat on the floor of the small rowboat that served as the *Scuabtuinne's* lifeboat, with three concerned faces staring down at him.

"Culloch?" he rasped. "You saved me?"

"Actually, you can thank Euan for that, Captain," Culloch replied, slapping the sodden apprentice on the shoulder. "He dived in after you."

"Joint effort, skipper," conceded Euan, his cheeks flushed. "Doyle threw the 'arpoon. He's a dab-hand with that thing."

"And just bloody missed me with it," croaked Macnia, lifting his weary body and plonking down on one of the boat's bench seats. He took another swig of the revitalising tea. "Seriously though, thank you, lads. Why'd you come back for me? I gave you clear orders."

"Bollocks to your orders," grunted Culloch. "We got halfway across, and we just couldn't do it. We couldn't just *leave* you, Skipper. We watched their ship go up in flames, so we turned back. I watched you dive into the sea, and you were headed right for us when you went under. It were Doyle here who saw that *thing* swimming after you. Moved like an eel, he said."

"Yeah, like an eel, skipper," Doyle confirmed. "Fast, like."

Macnia turned back and looked across the sea, where *El Caleuche* was now a raging, floating inferno, just in time to see her central mast come crashing down and dash what remained of her main deck into burning splinters. As the sun's orb crested the horizon, the mysterious ship faded from existence, leaving only a plume of rapidly dispersing smoke and the fragrant aroma of burning wood as evidence she had ever been there.

"What now, skipper?" asked Culloch.

"Now, we go back to the Scuabtuinne. I'm going to wash up, change my clothes, and then I'm going to get very, very drunk."

"So, just another normal day then?" grinned Culloch.

Macnia gave his chief tinker a cold look, then burst out laughing.

"Yes, just another day, Culloch."

***

Soon after, alone in his stateroom, Macnia pulled on a fresh jerkin and dried his hair on his musty, discoloured towel. He threw it down on the bed, snatched up the decanter of red wine and poured a generous measure into the pewter mug by his bedside. He raised it to his lips then hesitated as he caught sight of his reflection in the polished silver mirror above the basin opposite.

The previous twenty-four hours flooded through his mind in an instant: the terror, the pain, the confusion, the sorrow. Macnia sighed, his heart heavy as he contemplated Cardenas' fate. He dearly hoped *El Caleuche's* captain and crew had finally found their rest, freed from the chiloté's malevolent clutches. Many would not understand Cardenas' actions – how he had assisted those devils for so long. In Macnia's heart, he suspected he would have acted no differently.

And he knew, without Cardenas' help, he would be enslaved to that ship now: cursed to waylay other unsuspecting travellers and take them prisoner, all in the name of feeding those demons.

Macnia sighed, then wandered across to the head – the *Scuabtuinne's* single toilet, for the captain's exclusive use. He lifted the lid and, after a moment's hesitation, tipped the mug of wine into it.

There was nothing like almost dying to renew your zest for life, Macnia reflected. Perhaps it was time to start acting like a captain once more? He owed Cardenas that much.

But more, Macnia was obligated to his ship and his crew to be the best captain he could be.

El Caleuche

Above all, he owed it to himself.

End of Volume One

This is not the end… just *an* end.

Born of Inward Dreamings will return with its second volume, *Eldritch*, very soon. In the meantime, do not be afraid of the things in the darkness. If they've already noticed you, there's very little you can do about it.

*

Gareth Meadows is a British author who dabbles in the fantasy, Sci-Fi & dark comedy genres. Once described as 'This generation's Douglas Adams' (thanks Mum) and 'Hugely disappointing. A waste of your time and mine' (um… thanks Dad), he is currently endeavouring to translate the products of his feverish imagination into several novel, screenplay, and graphic novel projects.

His debut novel, 'Otherworld – The Heart of the Realm', is the first part in a fantasy trilogy, coming to all good book retailers when it finally finds its publishing home. You should follow him on Twitter – you won't not be disappointed.

www.otherworldtrilogy.com

twitter.com/GarethMeadows

Printed in Great Britain
by Amazon